T0158243

# IN A
# FOREIGN
# LAND,
# BY CHANCE

Nabaneeta Dev Sen

Translation by Soma Das

NIYOGI
BOOKS

*In a Foreign Land, by Chance:* English translation by Soma Das, of Bengali novella *Probashe Daiber Boshe* by Nabaneeta Dev Sen.

Published by

**NIYOGI BOOKS**

Block D, Building No. 77,
Okhla Industrial Area, Phase-I,
New Delhi-110 020, INDIA
Tel: 91-11-26816301
Email: niyogibooks@gmail.com
Website: www.niyogibooksindia.com

Original text © Nabaneeta Dev Sen
Translation © Niyogi Books

Editor: Jayalakshmi Sengupta
Design: Shraboni Roy

ISBN: 978-81-933935-1-2
Publication: 2017

Printed at: Niyogi Offset Pvt. Ltd., New Delhi, India

'Many things in East Europe reminded Bipasha of her country. After about five years in the West, she suddenly felt as though she had come closer to home. Yet, she couldn't put a finger on exactly where the similarity lay. The people were fair-skinned, the language was foreign and their politics too, was without substance. Socialist imperialism. Where then was the similarity? Bipasha could not identify it but could feel it. There were many unanswered questions yet...'

*- Chapter Two, p. 26*

# ONE

Pushing open the intricately carved, heavy wooden door, Bipasha stepped on to the gravelled pathway of the garden. To her right was a huge fountain, as usual adorned with customary nude fairies and, just as expected, dry. Bipasha quite liked it. How like her own country! Of late, in West Europe, she had become used to fully functioning, overflowing fountains. This bone-dry one, fascinated her. A dry fountain signified scarcity. The regal era of Budmerice Castle was now part of history, there could be no doubt. Like a lifeless dinosaur skeleton all that remained of it was its huge framework.

A red gravel path encircled the white stone castle, like an anklet around a foot. From it emerged several paths, radiating like sunrays drawn by a child. Cutting through the green garden, like thin slivers of a cake, they spread out in all directions.

One lead to a double-storied building to the left—the outhouse, perhaps. One disappeared into the apple orchard yonder. Although apple buds were yet to bloom, the orchard looked rather appealing. A peacock usually strutted there, in the orchard, happily sharing space with three turkeys. The day before, when the peacock spread its colourful tail, an abrupt and unplanned recess had interrupted their ongoing conference. Everyone had jostled for window space to catch a glimpse of the glorious sight. Now, Bipasha looked around for the peacock. She felt a kind of attachment with the bird. As though it was one of her own, from her own land. The peacock, amidst the flock of turkeys, was quite like Bipasha amongst these foreigners—starkly different. Another red path ran straight ahead and lost itself in the south-western woods.

That day was the final day of the writers' conference, and Bipasha was due to move on to some provincial town where another event awaited them. The group of young writers from foreign lands would visit various schools and colleges to make the acquaintance of their students.

But, before that, she needed to post a letter.

Bipasha chose the path that ran eastward, leading to the huge iron gates. Through the breaks in the foliage of the oak tree, she could see a guards' room. Armed guards were on duty—one stood by the room while two others stood guard on either side of the gates. Bipasha clutched the letter tight and walked ahead slowly. What a huge lock! The mammoth gates, each about as tall as two-and-a-half men, were held closed by a thick chain. In comparison, Bipasha herself could not even be considered of adult height!

As it was, things on the larger side always sent her heart fluttering and had anxiety bubbling within her. But the letter had to be posted. In the five or six days Bipasha had been in Czechoslovakia, she had not written home even once. Prior to that, while in England, she was extremely busy and did not find time to write. Her father, prone to anxiety, would surely worry himself sick. Bipasha just had to make a quick trip to the post office.

She reached the locked gates and looked around helplessly. The high gates, the large lock, the thick chain, the gun-toting guards—all these conspired to make her think that she was walking in the gardens of some prison. As though, any attempt to get the gates to open would be illegal. Her thoughts wandered... Samir, of course, had no chance of roaming at will. He lived alone in a hut; quite a different kind of life....

A wide paved road stretched beyond the gates. Bipasha looked to the east. The road was lined on both sides with rows of maple trees behind which fields rolled away. Saddled with poor eyesight, Bipasha tried to squint and sharpen her vision...grass fields or crops? From within the closed gates, it was hard to tell the difference between a grassy stretch and lush crops.

At the very end of the wide road, the sun rose like a roaring red war tank, armed for battle. Bipasha was hardly ever discomfited by situations. Especially when a close acquaintance—like the sun—was in sight. Moreover, the sun had put in a proper appearance after almost five days. She gathered back her vigour and walked up to the guards with a show of ease. Greeting one of them with a smile, she requested in English, 'Please would you be kind enough to open the gates?'

Although it was the Queen's language, without much scope for formal second-person address, as in her mother tongue, Bipasha's mind always switched to a formal mode when it came to the police. The guards said in unison, 'Guten morgen.'

But that was it! They displayed no signs of unlocking the gates. Bipasha's German was nothing to write home about, so she decided to try out her French and requested, 'Monsieur, would you be so kind as to unlock the gates?'

The guards smiled pleasantly and one of them replied in German, 'Yes, it is a splendid day.'

This made Bipasha break into an amused smile, dimpling her right cheek. The guards smiled back, giving Bipasha some courage. She walked up to the gates and rattled the lock. Then she said in her pure native Bengali, 'Moshai, please unlock the gates.' Holding up the letter she pointed to the road, saying, 'I have to go to the post office.'

Finally realisation dawned on the guards. They shook their heads and one of them said in German, 'Sorry, Frauline. That is impossible. You need permission.' And, in the next instant, they swiftly redirected their attention to the beauty and bounty of nature around. Bipasha understood...the gates would not open.

At her age, 'even bitches were beautiful' like they said back home, and Bipasha had a particularly lovely face. But alas, before abstemious castle guards, even a pretty face can fail miserably. Bipasha's mood soured. She would have to return, mission unaccomplished.

The moment she turned around, her eyes were dazzled by a sprawling stone castle—just like ones in the English fairy tales she had read in her childhood. A formidably shackled iron gate lay behind her and a towering castle in front. Budmerice. About 35 miles from Bratislava, this nineteenth century castle had now been turned to the official residence of writers from the state of Slovak, and called 'Writers' Home'.

Writers, academicians, and intellectuals of this land, whatever the topic of their written work—history, economics, social science, plays or fiction—were assured of free lodging, food and a peaceful environment for three months in this castle. No means of public transport served the place though. The travel to and from the castle was at the mercy of the government. Bipasha's thought to herself—The castle, the shackled gates, the landscaped gardens, the fountain, the peacock, the guards…and the captive princess. Now all that remained to complete the picture was a prince.

The thought made her laugh. A prince! Huh, what nonsense! The ones who were present in the castle were all young writers from various countries. Writers in real life rarely exhibited a sword-brandishing rebel streak. Their daredevilry was usually restricted to the tip of their pen.

But why was the castle so heavily guarded? What was the need? It was not as if the foreigners had much money on themselves. Before entering this land, they had to declare and settle all accounts. The little they had in their purses was the allowance granted by the government, and the only way to flee from there was on foot. Moreover, could anyone chain someone's soul? Samir was in prison. But was he really captive? Unlikely! The ones who want to break free, break free.

Lost in her thoughts Bipasha arrived at the rear of the castle. A huge, square reservoir with blue mosaic walls stood in front of her. It had a little water at its bottom with a dozen odd, red goldfish swimming in it. Bipasha leaned forward. 'Hey, haven't you frozen to death yet? Or don't you fear death till the water becomes ice?' she asked out loud.

'Actually, this reservoir is not meant for fish.'

Bipasha spun around, startled. She had been conversing to her heart's content with the fish, in Bengali. Well…looked like someone had caught her in the act.

Yohan, about one and half heads taller than her, leaned forward and explained, 'This used to be a swimming pool once, for the residents of the castle. Now, no longer in use.'

'Who said it is not in use? I can see it being put to good use! It is still a swimming pool. What do you think the goldfish are doing in there?'

'A swimming pool for fish…What a decadent imagination you have.' With a reverberating laugh Yohan stepped closer to see. It startled Bipasha and the fish too wiggled away. Could the fish hear from under the water? Did they get startled too?

Bipasha tried to move away a bit. Yohan's breath smelt of beer; the popular Czech beer—Pilsner. She had surely not said anything so very amazing that he had to trip and tumble all over her, showering his admiration

'Oh! What a splendid morning! exclaimed Yohan. 'Budmerice does not see such sun-soaked mornings very often.'

Oh dear! There he went…along the beaten track. Bipasha could easily predict what Yohan would say next. He would say, 'You are the bearer of this divine sunshine. It is your Indian charm that radiates in nature; the warm glow of your friendship that you carry everywhere.'

In the past five years, Bipasha had heard lines like these often enough to know them by heart. Alas, here lay the tragedy of human life. Rarely did one receive any well-deserved recognition for one's good deed. Yet, false praises were showered in abundance for achievements over which one had no claim, whatsoever.

Cutting off any possibility of a declaration along the lines of 'You are the golden morning…' Bipasha held out the letter towards Yohan and said, 'Yohan, your post office…?'

'Why? Do you need to post a letter? Give it to me.' Yohan took the letter from her and promptly posted it into the cavernous pocket of his overcoat. Bipasha was pretty and proportionate but on the smaller side. Whereas Yohan was on the larger side, very tall and slightly stooped, even for a Bengali girl, she was quite tiny-framed. The breast pocket of his coat beat Bipasha in height.

Bipasha raised her face towards that breast pocket and said, 'It hasn't got a stamp.'

'Ok, I will arrange for it. Airmail, right? Where to…India?'

'Hm. But Yohan, where is your post office?'

'Out there…about a mile and a half to the right, in the village.'

'But, the last meeting of the day starts in fifteen minutes. When will you go?'

'I won't go. I will give it to Bechka, she will put a stamp on it and drop it in the mailbag. Your letter will be on its way after lunch.'

'Thank you, thanks a lot. That's a relief!' Bipasha released a very audible sigh.

'Why are you so anxious? Who is the letter for? Your lover?'

'My lover?' As Bipasha laughed, Samir's face floated into her vision—the face from a photograph taken five years ago. Could she still call Samir her lover? In a preoccupied tone she called out Yohan's name to divert the conversation.

Instantly, from its great height, Yohan's made a rapid descent to hover near Bipasha's face—'Yes, ma chérie? Tell me, tell me…your words are like divine raga to my ears,' he said with a twinkle.

Though Bipasha had spent over five years in London, she was yet to come to terms with the

Western culture of grand and blatant flirting—the overt and intimate show of admiration to the fairer sex! Her face flushed and she forgot what she was about to say. Yohan's unselfconscious and impish ways reminded her of a childhood madcap book character, Pagla Dashu.

This Yohan was becoming a bit of a pest. Though he was a much respected professor in Bratislava and immensely popular at that—at the mere age of forty, he already had seven critical publications to his name and was the face behind the conference—yet, Bipasha felt, with his unkempt ways he was teetering towards lunacy. He liked to reserve a more than a fair share of attention for Bipasha. Perhaps, her petite frame was a matter of great delight to the six-feet-four Yohan. She was quite a misfit among the big-boned women of this region. Around Bechka she looked like an ethnic doll. Not only for her attire—a saree, and the long braid swinging down her back, or her tea-with-extra-milk complexion—there was in Bipasha's dark eyes a certain faraway, out-of-skin look.

After some thought, Bipasha came up with something to say, 'Is Bechka accompanying us to Nitra today?'

'Of course. Your interpreter is your shadow. How can she not come along? Well, it's a different matter that I would have liked very much to take Bechka's place...but I need to take care of some pending work here. I'll wrap it up quickly and join you in Nitra tomorrow. Till then Bechka will enjoy your company. The lucky girl!' Saying this, Yohan placed his warm and heavy hand on Bipasha's back and, bringing his face close to her ear, continued, 'Once I am in Nitra, I won't let Bechka come anywhere near you.'

Bipasha held her breath. Once again she caught the sweet pungent whiff of liquor. He was wearing tattered blue jeans and a short heavy black coat, with an inner lining of fur, its hood lying on his back. The corners of his eyes sported deep crow's feet—no wonder, because he smiled and laughed at the drop of a hat. He had a round face with a wide jawline and an aquiline nose. His smile appeared very familiar to Bipasha, but she could not dig up any memory of having seen it before. There was just this niggling thought that she had come across the smile before. For his age, Yohan had a sparse head of hair, though very shiny blonde. There was even a small bald patch at the back where the skin had been tanned by the sun to a coppery colour. His ever-smiling eyes were as clear as water.

For the past few days, Yohan had looked after everyone with extreme care and dedication. After all, catering to the needs of writers from around the world, with volatile tempers, was no mean feat.

What had worked wonders at this conference was its unique custom of bed-tea. It managed to soothe ruffled feathers early in the day.

Though the morning tea could not be technically called bed-tea, Bipasha preferred to do so. In fact, tea was not served in their rooms at all. After a quick wash, they had to gather in the dining room around half past seven in the morning. As soon as one was seated, a cup of black coffee and a measure of cognac would be served, with a basket of salted bread sticks on the side. Bipasha had no doubt, whatsoever, that it was this purifying rendezvous with cognac, the first thing in the morning, which filled the hearts of the writers with pristine joy. Nothing could match the hospitality of this country.

Bipasha Choudhury, writer and poet in the English language, was now a name to reckon with among readers of English literature. Yet, after five years of living in foreign lands, some native habits still remained ingrained in her. She did not mind a dash of cognac after dinner; what she could not bring herself to accept was this reckless indulgence early in the morning, almost straight out of bed!

And in the wake of that thought came the pangs of homesickness, the yearning for her city, Kolkata. Oh! How delighted her father and brothers would be if served with this Czech breakfast! This fulfilling breakfast would have surely upped the 'production capacity' of many writers back in her homeland! But alas, as luck would have it, instead of them it was Bipasha who was there.

Thanks to the cognac, everyone started the day in a cheerful mood. Whether the sun made an appearance or not, the gathering always shone bright. The daily events of the conference carried on peacefully, without a glitch. Bipasha noticed, how more than the novelists, the poets liked to play truant. The moment an opportunity arose, the poets skipped meetings and sauntered off into the woods.

'Would you like to go for a walk? Yohan asked. 'Come, let's go towards the woods.' Bipasha also observed how no one ever expressed a desire to take a walk towards the gate with its chains and locks. When they divided up into smaller groups, they always preferred the woods for a walk.

The day before, Bipasha too had gone for a walk toward the woods, with Hans, the East German poet. They had talked as they ambled along the red gravel path, which left the castle and cut through the green lawns. Where dry shrubbery, built up on either side the path, gradually headed towards the darkness of the woods.

Suddenly, Hans grabbed Bipasha's elbow and pulled her to a halt. He pointed to a spot under the shrubbery, where ripples were visible, beneath the covering of dry leaves on the ground. Surely, it was the covert movementof some animal, given away by the trembling leaves.

Bipasha cried, 'Snake!'

But Hans brushed her aside, 'No way! The winter hasn't passed yet...where will you find a snake? Must be a mongoose or something similar.'

Whatever the species, it surely did not move straight and narrow. It had a slithering gait. Hans's other hand had gone around her shoulder, like a half-moon, military-protection formation. They waited quietly in front of the woods—at the middle of the track.

A while later, when the leaves stopped trembling, Hans released Bipasha's elbow and said, 'Come on, let's go.' But Bipasha looked at her watch and realised that it was time for the next meeting. Hans though, made light of the matter and said, 'Oh come on, don't look at the time. We haven't even been into the woods.' From within the foliage of his facial hair, Hans's brown pair of eyes sought her out and pleaded, 'Please come with me to the woods.' And promptly, Bipasha's inner pair of eyes shot open and her senses screamed refusal, 'No, don't go. You must not go into the woods with Hans.'

Bipasha had not been able to throw caution to the winds. Panicked butterflies fluttered in her stomach as she said, 'Oh dear, I have to wrap up something before the meeting starts. I had completely forgotten…' She had taken flight and nearly sprinted back all the way to the sanctuary of the conference building. Away from Hans's pleading eyes. Who knows what lurked under the cover of dry leaves back there. No matter what Hans saw, Bipasha did see the slithering movement of an unseen snake.

Yohan again thumped her on the back and said, 'Come on beautiful, I'll show you the woods. It is truly worth a visit.'

Yohan's unmasked flirting did not make Bipasha nervous. It was assuring in some sense. Bipasha felt he would not take undue advantage after leading her into the woods. After all, barking dogs did not bite. So, having received permission from her instinct, Bipasha agreed and they set off in the direction of the woods, away from the red fish.

From somewhere, came the sound of loud barkings of dogs. Bipasha asked, 'Where is that coming from? Can't see any dogs around.'

Yohan replied, 'Well…they are close by. If you would like, I can show you the dogs first.'

A little ahead was the outhouse. From within it rose deafening growls of chained animals. The place looked as though it had been a stable at one time. Now, with the horses gone, the dogs were its masters. Above it, on the first floor balcony, some dirty clothes hung on a line, and an assortment of used utensils lay scattered.

'Whose dogs are these? And who lives on the first floor?' Bipasha asked curiously.

Yohan looked slightly uneasy, 'I don't really know. Perhaps castle employees…maybe the dogs, too, are theirs.'

Bipasha realised Yohan was feeling uncomfortable. At that moment, noticing an old man coming down the stairs, Yohan asked him about the dogs. The man replied in their native tongue. Yohan explained to Bipasha, 'The dogs belong to the castle.'

Bipasha did not really understand. Why did the castle own dogs? Wasn't the castle a government property itself? The dogs too, must then belong to the government. If so, for what purpose? The snarls and growls of the captive animals had shattered the calm of the new-born day. It was perhaps time to go into the woods. Bipasha set off on its trail. Yohan, strangely, seemed at a loss for words. With their ears still ringing with loud barking, they slowly walked into the forest.

Right from the place where the woods began, there were huge, tall trees. They wound and twisted around one another in a manner so as to keep the forest dark and the trapped forest air cool. Over time, unknown layers of moss had gathered on the tree barks. In contrast, budding new leaves peeked out from the branches. Unfamiliar and delicate creepers hung down from the trees, some had even started to flower. The chirps and twitter of birds stirred the still air of the woods with messages of the coming of spring. But, amazingly, the ground was not to be seen at all and Bipasha gazed in awe at the layer of snow covering it. A narrow path had been cut, over the snow-covered ground by pedestrians; a path smeared with sludgy snow and mud.

The amount of snow was quite surprising! It was true, though the calendar proclaimed that spring was here, it was still very chilly and the sun only made occasional appearances. Nevertheless, it had not snowed in the past few days. There was no trace of snow on the fields, lawns, paths, courtyards, balconies, or terraces of Budmerice Castle. Was it the sole responsibility of the woods to collect all the snow for safekeeping? Just outside the woods, the lush fields were awash with sunlight and shone bright green. Yet, a couple of steps into the woods brought one into a deep and dark wintry world of black and white. No matter what the calendar said, it was still winter within the woods.

Bipasha bent down and picked up a gloved handful of snow. Yohan was whistling an unfamiliar tune and, having armed himself with a rickety branch he had broken off, he was slicing through the hanging creepers.

'Yohan! Don't spoil the creepers, they are beautiful!' Bipasha reprimanded.

Yohan laughed. 'Spoil them? Come on…they will grow back by tomorrow. You are really sentimental, aren't you?. Is it possible to spoil a living, growing thing so easily? This is not art. This is a creation of nature.' Saying this, Yohan stuck the branch into the snow. It stood like a thin black pillar, crowned with odd straggly lengths of green creepers.

Yohan said, 'Let us say, this is the peak of a high mountain…perhaps a new peak of your great Himalayas. Today, this peak has been conquered for the first time, and we have done it…you and I.'

He looked at her with a soft gaze and holding her hand gently, said, 'Come, shall we plant the victory flag on it? Let these broken branches be the flag of our expedition team…what do you say? Saying this he placed his arm around Bipasha's shoulder and gently pulled her closer.

A scene flashed in Bipasha's mind—while coming down the stairs after a meeting, how Samir, for the first time, had…

Yohan broke into a laughter, disturbing Bipasha's trapped memories as well as the ageing foliage of the woods, frozen in time. Bipasha smiled quietly. 'Samir, see...see where I am now...lost in the woods...' Aloud she said, 'Come on Yohan, we'll be late for the last session.'

Yohan sighed, 'And now, the mountaineers start their descent from the peak.'

Quite abruptly, a strange silence filled the woods for a few moments. A heavy hush hung between Yohan and Bipasha. Bipasha felt an urgent need to break the silence, to say something, for some sound to shatter the stillness. But she could not. Instead, they started walking out of the woods.

Out in the green lawn, Bipasha found the peacock strutting around with its three turkey companions. It appeared to be playing in the field by the apple orchard, swaying its blue green feathers. A migrant peacock. Possibly, a lonely peacock.

'Don't you feel cold? How do you manage in this extreme cold and snow?' Bipasha asked the peacock. 'Don't you feel homesick? Don't you realise that these are turkeys? They are not of your kind...there isn't another peacock here....'

She was carrying on this silent conversation with the peacock when Yohan pointed to it and said, 'Look Bipasha, one of your own. Another beautiful bird from India.'

—◄o►—

# Two

'Evichka, look! Look how dangerously Bipasha is chewing on chillies!' Yohan shrieked. 'Be careful! Don't eat so many. Alas, you know not what you do! You'll be ruined, I tell you. You'll feel the chillies twice, once now and again tomorrow morning…' And he broke into a guffaw like a naughty little boy.

'Yo-ha-an!' Elizabeth and Eva, as Evichka was often called, scolded him in unison. 'What kind of indecency is this? That too, in front of ladies!'

'Huh! As if Yohan cares for decency! He is a barbarian. Just look at his attire…what a filthy pair of trousers.'

'Truly, your clothes are the worst in this restaurant, Yohan.'

'But Bipasha's attire makes up for mine completely…isn't that so, Bipasha?' The dishevelled

Yohan, in his tattered blue jeans, cast a very intimate gaze towards Bipasha.

Bipasha pondered, perhaps the gold thread flowers on her green Mysore-georgette saree were shining a bit too brightly in the dim setting of the huge candlelit room. There was no doubt that the restaurant had seen better days as a very posh place. The wood panelling on the walls and the chandeliers hanging from the ceiling stood proof of those times. There were six of them sitting around a table, covered with a starched white tablecloth—Bipasha, Yohan, Eva, Elizabeth, Danish, and Gjorge. A lone daffodil graced the table in a narrow-necked, cut-glass vase. Beside it was a basketful of different types of dry breads. At each end of the table was a silver candelabrum holding aloft a pair of lit candles. And in front of them were wide-mouthed crystal glasses; some filled with a swirling red liquid and others with water-clear vodka. Yohan was in charge of attending to these. There were two cut-glass bowls filled with small round, red and green chillies; one bowl had fresh ones while the other had ones soaked in vinegar.

The sudden sighting of fresh chillies pulled at Bipasha's heart strings, and she promptly chewed up a couple with some bread. And that was what triggered Yohan's brazen and immature dig at her. Bipasha had heard this kind of wit only from her brothers within the four walls of their home in Kolkata—nowhere else, neither in Europe nor in her own country. She had almost forgotten about such humour in the past five years.

She could not let the comment wash over her as easily as Eva and Elizabeth did. A pang of homesickness shot through her heart, for the playfully crude camaraderie of her brothers, for her own land, for the hours the three siblings had spent chatting at the dining table. She hadn't seen them in ages. How much longer would it be? But how and where could Bipasha return? How would she face that political party? The police? Samir was still in prison. How would she face him? Samir was living with a misunderstanding. But Samir, it is not the way you think....

'This is a Hungarian restaurant so today we are having Hungarian food.' Danish said and then exclaimed, 'Here! Here comes our goulash!'

Big bowls of thin gravy, which had taken on the colour of red chillies, arrived, loaded with chunks of beef, potatoes, and tomatoes.

'Goulash is Hungary's...' Danish started to explain but Bipasha cut him off mid-way and said, 'main and perhaps the only food. Right? We know that much because goulash is very popular in West Europe too. The Hungarian food is quite familiar, but we are yet to taste any of your native food.'

'What are you saying? Have you not tasted the flavours of Czech or Slovak food in the past week?'

'How could we? You have been feeding us only Viennese, French, and Hungarian. And today, the last meal happens to be Hungarian. Are your Czech and Slovak dishes unfit to be served to guests?'

'Oh dear, very true! Bechka, Evichka...is this how you have looked after Bipasha?'

Bipasha noticed the discomfiture on Eva and Elizabeth's faces, and suddenly she felt ashamed. How could she blame these people? After all, when she and her people entertained guests in Kolkata, did they ever take the guests to roadside eateries for meals of local fare? Of course not, the guests were taken to proper restaurants with much pomp and flair for meals of foreign cuisine like Mughlai and Chinese. Or perhaps, to taste food from other regions of India like Punjab or the South. These Czechs and Slovaks too, were in a similar situation. Having realised this, Bipasha said,

'We Bengalis too, are quite like you. We don't serve guests our everyday food. Instead, we try to impress them with foreign cuisine. And, in course of that, we fail to understand that we are actually depriving our foreign friends of the local taste.'

'Oh forget it!' Eva said to Bipasha aside. 'Don't feel deprived. Slovak cuisine is poor man's food, and there is nothing called Czech culinary delicacy in the world. Perhaps, you would have found some restaurants in Prague, serving Czech food for tourism purposes, but don't expect anything in this godforsaken rural region.'

Yohan said, 'Well, the purpose was to feed the guest good food. The French, the Viennese, and the Hungarians cook well. We make good cut-glass stuff...and, of course, good beer. Evichka, please tell Bipasha what else we do well.'

'We make love well.' Gjorge quipped abruptly, in German.

Gjorge, the poet, was by nature a quiet and shy person. And, unlike Eva, Elizabeth, and Danish, he was not a student of the language school. These three were students of Yohan, while Gjorge was his friend. He was a reserved, clean shaven, young, usually dressed in white shirt, wide black tie, and black suit.

By appearance he could easily be mistaken for an officer of some foreign bank.

Quite strangely, there were no couples at the dinner party. Though, except for Bipasha and Elizabeth, the others had all tied the knot at some point of time. Evichka's body proudly proclaimed her 'good news'. Danish, dressed in a grey suit, dark blue shirt, and red tie, looked like a boy himself; but, in reality, he was a father of two.

Yohan was married too. He had two sons and his aged mother lived with him. Gjorge had been married in the past but was a free bird now. Though he claimed expertise in the area of romance, Bipasha doubted his capabilities because he seemed to be more interested in Yohan.

On the other hand, Elizabeth's body was a proud declaration to the world of its youth and appeal. Elizabeth was of large build and her physical bounty seemed to crave release from the confines of clothing like a bullet from a gun. Her skin was rosy from the rush of blood beneath; yet, she liked to use a lot of make-up on her face. Her tall and broad frame and her sensual appeal reminded one of the ancient Scandinavian goddesses. She had shiny blonde hair, cascading down her back, blue tinged irises, thick eyelashes, and flushed red cheeks and lips.

Elizabeth and Bechka were farm girls, always smiling brightly, like those in toothpaste commercials.

Elizabeth was dressed in a micro-mini skirt and all eyes were at liberty to travel up her thighs, right up to their juncture. She reminded one of a military tank, armed with a double cannon to take on the field, ready for war. In fact, Bipasha felt a little embarrassed, each time she looked up. Her gaze was drawn to her ample bare flesh like a crow eyeing the dead. Funnily, though, the mini skirt was no longer in vogue in West Europe.

Eva, Danish, and Bechka were secretaries at the conference. Eva was a Jewish girl with black hair falling in layers to her shoulders; the only interesting feature on her paper-blank face was her pair of dark and bright eyes, which sparkled when she laughed. She wore a maternity smock and was the complete contrast of Elizabeth. But, Eva was the one who spoke well. Though by appearance she was quite unnoticeable, her soft voice usually made her presence felt.

Bipasha couldn't help noticing one fact though— girls of this nation preferred to push the men upfront and remain in the background. At the lecture, it was only the men who raised questions—the ladies remained comparatively quiet, just listening.

That evening Bipasha was being given a formal farewell. Bipasha noticed how none of the men had brought their wives, though in West Europe to attend such social dos as a couple was the norm. Eva's husband was, of course, out of town; away in Prague for a couple of months. And Elizabeth was still looking for one. Though her blazing sensuality was a huge challenge for all males of the world, by nature she was quite timid and shy, blushing to the roots of her hair at the drop of a hat.

Yohan was the only one who indulged in unabashed flirtation with Bipasha. But even though Danish did not flirt, Bipasha noticed how his mesmerised gaze made her conscious of her femininity. As for Gjorge… well, Bipasha had a strong hunch that he was least interested in the womankind. Yohan was the man Gjorge worshipped—Bipasha could almost see fumes of holy incense arising from his gaze.

But Yohan did not seem to be bothered by it at all. He was busy keeping Eva, Elizabeth, and Bipasha entertained, simultaneously. Bipasha observed that Eva and Elizabeth were furtively amused at this.

Yohan's teasing flirtatiousness had an honest manliness, a certain sweet, naughty, innocuous, childlike charm about it.

Perhaps it was due to Yohan's overwhelming personality that Gjorge and Danish had receded into a shadowy existence. Yet, earlier today, Danish was Bipasha's day-long companion. He was studying Sanskrit and had asked Bipasha for a pocket-sized Gita in Sanskrit. He had pulled out a small English Gita from his shirt pocket and shown it to Bipasha. Danish was equally fluent and proficient in English, French, German, Russian and now, Sanskrit.

Yohan had made a wrong assumption in the gardens of Budmerice Castle. Since coming to Nitra, it was not Bechka but Danish who had been acting as Bipasha's interpreter. But, this afternoon, while Bipasha was delivering her lecture to the students, Yohan arrived like a strong gust of wind—Bipasha was alerted of his arrival by the tremor of excitement and flurry that ran through the students in the hall.

Here, Yohan was a celebrity of sorts. And with his arrival, Danish had become part of the wallpaper. In the past two days, Bipasha and Danish had talked a lot. When Bipasha asked to see photographs of his children, Danish had been at a loss. Had he been a father from West Europe or the USA, he would have swiftly flipped open his wallet and displayed a perfect family photograph. But Danish was not able to pull that off. He said, 'Photo? Where will I get a photo? Those are at home.' Bipasha liked his reply. What a relief…this meant that they lovingly saved the photos of their wives and children in their hearts, not in their wallets. Quite like India.

Many things in East Europe reminded Bipasha of her country. After about five years in the West, she suddenly felt as though she had come closer to home. Yet, she couldn't put a finger on exactly where the similarity lay. The people were fair-skinned, the language was foreign and their politics too, was without substance. Socialist imperialism. Where then was the similarity? Bipasha could not identify it but could feel it. There were many unanswered questions yet.

The entire concept of social imperialism was quite vague to Bipasha. Her party too, had never enlightened the members about it. Bipasha had been awed to find that the party's views for Hungary-Czechoslovakia differed from its views regarding Tibet. One was 'occupation' while the other was 'liberation'. Why? Because in one, socialism had already existed, while in the other, it had not. Was that it? The party did not answer many of her questions. All it did was vent out noxious views regarding communism in Europe. At the time, Albania was not counted as part of East Europe, because the country was loyal to Peking.

In the past five years, Bipasha had given the matter much thought—the party had instilled wrong ideas in her, it had led her to believe in many biased and incomplete notions. Surely, East Europe was much better.

This was Bipasha's first visit to a non-capitalist nation. Certainly, it would not be as bad as she was expecting! To be honest, her understanding of politics was not something to applaud. In Samir's proximity she had comprehended quite a bit; on her own, she was at a loss. For the past few years, her solitary life in Europe had taught her a lot. She had learnt to think for herself and develop a perspective different from Samir's. And, due to that, she had gradually come to understand the problems plaguing her own country. She had realised where the party was going wrong. Would she have gained this realisation if she had not travelled abroad? Who knows!

'Danish, come let's head towards the office now,' Yohan said as he offered them caramel custard.

Caramel custard? Again? Bipasha's mood plummeted. Then, suddenly, the word 'office' grabbed her attention. Why office? 'What do you mean by that? Are you going to work so late?' Bipasha asked.

Yohan laughed aloud at her surprise; Danish answered, 'Yes, we have to work. Very important work. You all will come along as well. Do you think the lavish dinner was for free? Don't you have to repay in some way? Slog a little?'

Seeing Bipasha completely baffled, Eva, Elizabeth, and even Gjorge started to laugh.

Gjorge said, 'Yohan, I am not coming. I have a cold and it is raining today. I don't want to stay out late. It also looks like it might rain.'

Yohan scolded Gjorge and, unable to reach his back, thumped Evichka's instead, just because the poor girl happened to be closer to him.

'Gjorge, don't be a wet blanket…you are becoming a nuisance. You call this rain? It's just a drizzle without which spring can never set in. I'll give you a shot of strong liqueur…your cold will vanish and your head will be set ablaze! Everyone will come to my office now.

Squad, attention!' Saying that, he promptly jumped up
to stand in attention himself.

The other clients at the restaurant kept looking at
the charming lunatic with a smile on their face.

Danish explained to Bipasha with a smile, 'There
is a well-stocked cellar in Yohan's office. Actually, it can
be called his public-relations office. That is where we
are headed.'

They left the restaurant and started to walk.
It was drizzling, and the roads were devoid of trams
and buses.

'Shall I call a cab? Can you walk?' Danish asked.

'Ask Evichka instead,' Bipasha said. 'She might...'

'Of course not. I can walk very well. The doctor
has asked me to walk,' Eva cut in.

They came to a road, which was in near darkness
and flanked by tall buildings on either side. The lamp
posts tried their best to cast some light on the wet
cobblestone road but without much success. Bipasha
was very fond of these cobbled roads. The buildings
along the road were also in darkness except for a few
lighted rooms. These buildings were of the university,
now closed. Hence the neighbourhood had been
plunged into darkness.

The road was empty except for their small procession, which abruptly came to a halt outside the huge locked doors of a palatial building. The words 'Music School' were written on its wall in large lettering. Yohan stood in front of the doors and rummaged through his pockets. His coat alone had about ten pockets, inside, outside and all around! He came up with a notebook, a pipe, a lighter, matchsticks in abundance, a handkerchief, a story book even, pens, pencils, and quite a few bunches of keys—some for his house, some for his office in Bratislava, and some for the party office. Yohan was the first secretary of the local chapter of the communist party. Eventually, the keys for the building were dug out from the well of his trouser pocket and the doors to Music School opened.

Bipasha and the rest pushed open the doors of Music School and got inside. Gjorge made one last attempt to flee but had to discard the idea in the face of Danish's protest and Yohan's reproach.

The staircase was huge and the walls were plastered with myriad publicity posters. Apparently, the place hosted various cultural shows. There were posters advertising piano recitals, operas, and theatres alongside folk dances and folk music. Bipasha glanced at the posters as she climbed the marble staircase to the first floor. She tilted her head back to look at the ceiling. It was designed as nested domes, held up by massive pillars. Their party of six reached the first floor, and they stood in a long, deserted corridor, which bridged the cavernous stretches of darkness at either end. In front was a huge blackboard on which various instructions had been written in chalk. To Bipasha, they were as indecipherable as the lines of destiny etched by the Almighty on her forehead.

Yohan started off towards the left, and the group followed. Light from the street lamps found occasional gaps to shine through on the corridor, creating long shadows of the mammoth pillars.

Suddenly, they heard a voice say in protest, 'No!' A female voice. 'Ne!' This was followed by a pleading male voice…the words were muffled. The female voice again cried, 'Ne Ne Ne!'

Among the six pairs of feet, three had stopped in their tracks. Bipasha, Eva, and Elizabeth stood silently, but Yohan marched on. Danish and Gjorge followed, with uncertainty in their footsteps.

All of a sudden, a girl ran into view from behind the wall, her hands covering her face. Her hair and the tail of her coat, flying in disarray. She stopped abruptly in the corridor and removed her hands, and immediately her gaze fell on the group.

Yohan exclaimed, 'Yana! What's up?'

Yana wagged her index finger and tried to lodge a complaint with Yohan. At that moment, another man walked into sight, laughing as he came towards them. Something flashed in his hands and a spark of light lit up the corridor making its darkness all the more prominent. The girl screamed again, 'Ne, Karl!'

Karl's loud laughter echoed in the corridor as he said, 'Thank you, Yana.' He held in his hands a children's camera, complete with a flashbulb.

Gosh! So this was what it was! Eva and Bechka dissolved into giggles. Then Eva said, 'Karl, you will get many opportunities to click Yana. Why don't you take a few snaps of Bipasha today?'

Karl advanced with his camera saying, 'Of course, why not? That is...if she has no objections. Phew! The way Yana was screaming, anyone would have thought that having found her alone in this deserted building I was attempting to dishonour her!'

'And that is exactly what we thought,' Eva said.

Bechka added with an abashed smile, 'What fools we are!'

Karl was extremely handsome. He walked up to Bipasha and requested with his head bowed, 'May I?'

Like a bolt out of the blue, Yohan rushed into the scene and interrupted, 'All six of us will be in the photo…and yes, Yana too.' Saying that, he pulled Yana into the circle.

Karl clicked a group photo and then said, 'Now a single, of the lady in the saree.'

Bipasha felt terribly embarrassed. As it was, they had walked in on an intimate moment of these two lovers, spoiling their time. And now, in this dark, massive and deserted corridor they were asking him to click photos for them. She found the whole affair meaningless. Of what use were photographs? Could one hold on to a person forever through a photograph? Could a photograph capture a soul forever?

Karl made Bipasha lean against a pillar. He even expressed a desire for her to take her coat off, but Bipasha refused. A bone-chilling wind was blowing into the corridor and she had no desire, whatsoever, to freeze to death while advertising her saree. As soon as he had clicked her, Karl asked for her address.

Yohan snubbed him with a scold, 'What will you do with her address? Give it to me when it's ready, I'll send it to her. Just remember Yana's address…that should do for you.'

At this everyone broke into a laughter. After saying goodbye repeatedly, and in various ways, Karl and Yana walked away together, disappearing into the darkness towards the other end of the corridor—side by side, but surprisingly, without their arms around each other.

'What were they doing in this locked building, so late at night?'

'Karl teaches music in the Music School, and Yana is a graduate student here. They must have been rehearsing in some part of this sprawling building,' Bechka explained.

Bipasha thought about how they hadn't even held hands while walking away. Yet, it was quite evident that they were lovers. This was so much like her own country. On the contrary, public behaviour of lovers in West Europe was quite the opposite. But, in the next instant, Bipasha felt that it wasn't like her country. In her land, lovers did not hold hands because of the orthodox mindset of society. While here, the reason was progress. In both places, one wouldn't come across vulgar display of sexuality; in her country it was because society was yet to reach that moment of release, while here that moment had come and passed long back. After all, the communist discipline was very different.

She wondered how much truth there was in all those negative views about East Europe and its socialistic imperialism, which their party had instilled in them. Revisionism and its reaches was not easy to fathom and, yet, it was true that the young people here showed more restraint—they had an ideology to follow—whatever that was, it was surely better than the capitalist mentality of West Europe.

Back in her country, all that Bipasha had learnt in the name of communism were Mao's maxims. Ironically, in the last five years, all she had done was set up camp in foreign lands and feed off her father. And yes, become an Indian writer who wrote in English. This conference was, of course, an outcome of the same.

Many changes had crept into Bipasha in the course of her stay abroad. Now she could somewhat understand the workings of communism in Italy and France. Back home, all she had reserved for them was hatred. This visit was, however, her first entry behind the Iron Curtain. Surprisingly, she couldn't fathom much. There seemed to be a layer of mist shrouding everything, just the way the rest of the world thought this place to be. Overall, the impression that one could gather, hardly erased doubts or brought relief. Instead of the satisfaction of everyone having everything and the contentment of being a resident of a classless society, there was a peculiar tension which held everyone taut.

Bipasha thought—had Samir been here in my place he would have gauged the situation far better. I don't understand these things very well. My mind is filled with numerous questions...all unanswered. But then, Samir would never have come to Czechoslovakia in the first place. This was a big drawback of their party. The way it created mental barriers; the way it did not allow the mind to open its doors. The East European countries made a big deal about borders in order to save their nations from bourgeois infiltration. In the same way, their party too had drawn strict mental boundaries for them to save their minds from bourgeois infiltration. Difficult to ascertain what is right! Isn't it necessary to erect a fence around a sapling when it is growing?

Of late, Bipasha's mind had opened all its doors and windows; done away with its boundaries.

She found it very hard to anchor her mind. Often she felt, this is right…but that could also be right. Was it alright to be so broadminded? Could this be called broadmindedness or was it a weakness? Or was it lack of faith? How novel would it be to brand the lack of commitment as liberalism! Was Samir then narrow-minded? And was that the reason why he awaited justice behind bars, for the last five years? Well, all said and done, Samir too, would have never held her hand in public.

'Bipasha, what's wrong? You seem to be completely immersed in the night scene. What is so interesting here?' Danish walked up and stood beside her, resting his elbows on the railing. Bipasha was stirred from her reverie. She was standing in the shadow of a massive pillar holding on to the railing. In the light from a street lamp she could see the bushy crown of a tree getting drenched in the drizzle. The wind played with her hair, whipping it around her face.

'Yohan's party is probably already halfway through…'

'Of course not,' Evichka interrupted. 'Yohan has just about managed to unlock the door and switch on the light.'

They walked to Yohan's reception room. There was a very old fashioned yet splendid looking couch set in dark blue and yellow. Various pieces of furniture in mahogany wood surrounded it—a heavy round table, thick shelves laden with books. There was a glass pot from which creepers rose and the floor was covered in a plush carpet.

Through the open connecting door, Bipasha saw Yohan in the adjoining room. The room had furniture made of walnut wood, in a very contemporary style. Quite clearly, it was the office room. She saw Yohan opening a cabinet and soon, soft clinks of cut-glass crockery filled the room. Yohan appeared to have conjured up a considerable number of bottles in various shapes and sizes. A thought flashed through Bipasha's mind—in what way was this any different from any bourgeois drinking do? Oh dear, why did these silly thoughts have a tendency to find place and perch within her mind?

There could be no ground for comparison between the Hindu-Muslim social structure of India and the Christianity influenced social ways of the West. Moreover, norms of hospitality were usually unique to every country. Bipasha pulled herself up for giving in to prejudiced thoughts. Weren't guests welcomed with grand banquets in communist Peking? Even for Nixon?

Yohan and Danish were busy filling up the glasses. Gjorge stood by the bookcase, flipping through the odd book every now and then. Bechka and Evichka were away, on a short visit to the washroom; Bipasha had already declined an invitation for the same. Evichka, in her condition, needed to answer the call of nature very frequently, and Bechka liked to touch up her lip colour almost as often.

Bipasha preferred to stay away from make-up. She too, wanted to flip through the books but they were all in Czech or Slovak. Besides, she was not at all keen to be in Gjorge's proximity. His demeanour clearly proclaimed an aversion to womankind, and that had pricked Bipasha's self-respect. Hence, in want of better things to do, Bipasha consigned herself to watching Yohan's and Danish's ritual of preparing the drinks.

'Ice?' Bipasha asked.

'Where will I get ice so late?' Yohan replied.

'Why? Isn't there an ice machine around here? Or a refrigerator?'

'Refrigerator? Ice machine!' Yohan guffawed.

Danish then asked, 'What did you think this place to be? New York? Or Chicago?'

Bipasha felt embarrassed, 'Oh no…but…'

Yohan cut in, 'No buts. Those are luxuries of the capitalist world. The fact that we have hard drinks is more than enough.'

Surprisingly, Bipasha could not detect any strain of idealistic pride in the words. On the contrary, was there a hint of regret in there?

At that moment, the huge wooden door was thrown open…without any warning knocks. A stocky and bull-necked figure, though not very tall, walked in. He wore only a pullover to battle the extreme cold…no coat! He held a red earthenware tub close to his chest with both hands. No gloves either! Four bright red tulip buds peeked out of the tub from among a cluster of frail green leaves.

Bipasha gaped in amazement and wondered, how did he manage to turn the door knob if both his hands were occupied?

The young man burst into the room like a rush of spring and hollered, 'Yo-ha-an!'

In the meantime, 'the mystery of the opening door' was solved. Bechka and Evichka had held the door open for him. They now followed him into the room and took their seats. By then, the young man had raised quite a ruckus in the native language. Here was one person who could give away Yohan's tongue to the cat!

Eva informed, 'Mirko. Madunichki Mirko... a very popular playwright. His plays are acted out by the professional theatre groups. He likes to experiment a lot through his plays...also delves into old folklores.'

'Madunichki Mirko.'

Bipasha jumped as the man swiftly dropped to his knees at her feet, holding the tulip tub in his hands. Tulips were spring flowers and usually bloomed in April. Bipasha suddenly realised that the flower tub was being offered to her!

Mirko showered her with a long speech in the unfamiliar tongue and his eyes sparkled with humour as he spoke.

'Mirko doesn't speak English. He is saying that today, he confers the title of Spring Queen on you... you are the prettiest among us. If you accept the flowers then he will be extremely gratified.'

Bipasha felt as though everyone in the room was greatly enjoying her abashed state. But, to be honest, she did not like being repeatedly singled out and labelled 'the prettiest' in the presence of other girls. In West Europe, such a thing would not have happened.

Etiquettes and practices were far more subtle, much more mature there and sentiments of others were always taken into consideration by everyone.

Eva might not take offence…after all, her victory trophy was residing in glory beneath her smock. But what about Bechka? Though very beautiful, she was yet to find a suitor. She had confided in Bipasha once that she did not want passing lovers; she was looking for a perfect husband. Unfortunately, she was yet to cross paths with someone of her liking.

Bipasha had already relieved Mirko of the flower tub, even before her interpreter had finished explaining. Now, she stood up to look for a suitable place to deposit the tub.

And immediately, the room was startled by Mirko's awed and sharp intake of breath. Still on his knees, he adopted a dramatic pose—hands outstretched, upper body leaning back and mouth open in an awe-struck 'O'—and launched into a breathless rendition of a string of never-before-heard words.

Amidst the laughter that ensued, Danish interpreted, 'O Spring Queen, had you not risen to your feet, I would have remained deprived of the full extent of your beauty…a spring fairy, a green grasshopper.'

And, halfway through the flattery, Bipasha realised with shock that she had left the ground and was hanging in mid-air, her feet kicking about aimlessly. Mirko's hard and rough hands were now clasping her instead of the flower tub and, having lifted her off the ground, he was spinning her around. Quite clearly, Bipasha's preference or permission was of no significance here!

Mirko was singing in his baritone voice and, from the typical tune, Bipasha guessed it to be some folksong. And then, when he came to a particular line, everyone joined in. Bipasha couldn't make head or tail of the lyrics. All she could do was remain suspended with the budding tulips clasped to her bosom and a head of dark brown hair blocking her vision. Had the flower tub not kept her hands engaged, she would have surely yanked out a handful of that hair.

What a frightfully spirited young man! She started to feel angry at herself, for being so petite. At the same time, a thought coursed through her mind—it was as though the brightness of youth had ripped apart a tattered and stained curtain to suddenly light up the room. After about three or four twirls, Mirko reached the end of his song. He then put Bipasha down and, after relieving her of the flower tub, deposited two very warm and smacking kisses on her palms.

Bipasha's head was caught in a twister. Such melodrama did not agree with her and she flopped down on the sofa. Her head reeled. Samir, you are so thin…you would never be able to twirl me around this way! Would you? Samir, Samir….

'Gosh! Mirko, what's happening? Can't you see she is as fragile as a little bird? How could you subject her to such assault?' Yohan scolded and offered Bipasha a drink.

Without caring to enquire about the nature of the drink, Bipasha was about to accept the glass when Mirko swooped upon it like a gush of wind and snatched it away. Then he held the glass to Bipasha's lips and recited a few lines from some poetry in his absolutely incomprehensible language, adoration dripping from his voice. The room again erupted in loud laughter.

Bipasha couldn't really bring herself to be angry. Mirko's smiling face was quite a misfit for his giant frame. His neck was stocky and reminded her of a bull. Yet, his face was bursting with the naïve lustre of youth. He couldn't be over twenty-five, about the same age as Bipasha.

Lost in these thoughts, Bipasha sipped her drink and almost choked as the fiery vodka burned a path down her throat. Mirko took the glass from her with a display of much humility and sipped from it.

This time, Bechka, Eva, and Danish scolded him in unison, 'Why are you finishing off the poor girl's drink? Don't you have one of your own?'

'The drink in this glass is surely far more intoxicating…a witness to friendship…' Mirko said in fluent French and winked.

'What! You know French and have not been speaking for so long?' Bipasha was stunned.

'He knows quite a few more languages. We all know Hungarian, of course…in Slovakia, someone or the other in every family is from Hungary. We also know German…and those who are into literature make the effort to learn French…' Danish said.

All of a sudden, something struck Bipasha's mind and she cut off Danish, saying 'And Russian… everyone here knows Russian, isn't that so?'

Mirko replied, 'Ruski? Ne, ne!' Then he switched to French, 'None of us know Russian. Do we? Yohan? Danish? Evichka? Gjorge? Do we know Russian?'

Yohan cut him off with some serious-sounding words in a very grave voice. And, immediately, an argument erupted between them. Quite a heated and serious argument in which Gjorge also contributed his bit. Danish, Eva, and Elizabeth listened in silence. In a while, Eva explained to Bipasha, 'It's about politics. Sometimes Mirko says things he shouldn't say in public. Yohan is trying to warn him off, and that's what the fight is about.'

Danish chipped in, 'Yohan is right. Mirko can be very childish.'

Elizabeth said, 'Actually, being an artist, Mirko is not always aware of reality. He lives in a world of his own.'

'Uh-huh!' Elizabeth objected, 'Gjorge is also an artist, but he is very much aware of reality.'

Danish said, 'It is not about being an artist…it has more to do with individual personality. Moreover, the concept that artists are whimsical is a purely bourgeois-made pretence. A clever way of acquiring a social licence to exercise free will and ways. Is an engineer in any way less creative than a poet? Or is he less important in society? How come no one pardons an engineer's slipups by branding those as an artist's whims?'

Bipasha felt as if she was hearing Samir speak. They had argued in exactly the same way. Were

poets and artists more important than engineers
and doctors? Was a plate of food more necessary or
a page of poetry? In the then economic and social
scenario of India, the answer was clear to them. But in
the past five years, such things had become quite
muddled for Bipasha.

Samir had just been sent behind bars when
Bipasha's father forcibly packed her off to Mumbai,
and then to England from there. That was the time
when things started to fall out of perspective.

Samir, you will not understand...I know, you will
not believe that I did not run away. I was truly not at
fault. I did not have the strength to stand up against
my powerful father. And because of that...because
of that incapacity, today my entire being, my mind is
peeling away like the trunk of a date palm. Look at
me, Samir! Thorns...I am studded with thorns, Samir!
Do you know, Samir, who this Bipasha really is? What
she is about? The same Bipasha...your Bipasha! She
now lives in London and writes poetry in English.
What can be more decadent than this? Samir...Samir,
I know, you despise me. I know, I know, I know....

'Actually, we all know Russian,' Eva said. 'They
teach us in school. The way you learn English in
school...kind of similar.' She added with a short laugh.

Bipasha returned to the reality of the room with a startle. Danish was offering her another drink while Yohan remained completely engrossed in the argument. Eva's words had answered many of her questions. Especially, her curiosity at the way Mirko had said, 'Ruski? Ne, ne!' The hazy image of socialist imperialism started taking definite form. Language! Of course. Wasn't that the primary weapon of imperialism? Forceful introduction into a different culture and thought path through the medium of language. Else, how would the brainwash be possible? Now Bipasha understood what the argument was all about and why.

Yohan was the first secretary of the local chapter, and he had some official responsibilities. He surely had the authority to prune such irresponsible statements. Was then Yohan part of the establishment? But his attire told a different story. The others wore ties, except for Mirko, who was in a turtle-neck pullover. Surprisingly, beneath his coat, Yohan was dressed in a green shirt whose top buttons were undone to reveal curious tufts of blonde chest hair peeking and winking at Bipasha. The hems of his blue jeans were threadbare, in tatters and muddy.

The room was quite warm, perhaps centrally heated. The men had shed their jackets and roamed in their shirts. Danish had even asked for permission to take off his tie.

Gjorge was drinking away, lost in his own realm of thoughts. This silent man was the only one here who hailed from Bipasha's world. Another poet. The thought sent a shiver of repulsion through Bipasha. Since the time she arrived here, the absurdity of being an Indian poet in the English language had become extremely prominent to her. She felt as though these people were having a laugh behind her back. 'Alas! A victim of colonial imperialism. Ignorant of her mother tongue, she is dedicated to the creation of artificial literary art in the language of her oppressor.' Though no one had yet said so in as many words, Bipasha was sure their thoughts travelled that path. Even Gjorge's.

Bipasha thought to herself—Gjorge, had I written poetry in Bengali, you wouldn't have disregarded me in this manner. To be honest, the lot of you regard me as quite unimportant. As an international writer, I should receive extra credence and respect; you should be happy that you can read and enjoy my writing. But, quite contrarily, you think of me as the moon…not the sun. I have no light of my own; I am trying to be a language artist with borrowed light. I know, you pity me. And this is another instance where you are very similar to my countrymen. And different from the West.

It is only because I write in English that today I am a 'writer'. Don't I know that there are writers who pen far better poetry than I do? But, because they write in Bengali, their names will never feature anywhere in the West. They will not find place in the Oxford Book of Verse. No one will ever see them or hear of them in the Indian Literature course in universities. But I will be there. Bipasha Choudhury will be in all these places.

I will be there because I have written 'My Vindhya Nods'. I will be there because I have written 'The Circe Song'. But, Samir, no one will know of you. No one will know about the poetry you are writing during your days of imprisonment. No one will care whether you are writing at all. Of course, Gjorge would have paid you attention. I loathe Gjorge.

Mirko's mood had soured completely. Yohan was still at him. After a while, Bechka suddenly walked up and stood between them. Then she said something which made Yohan grind to a stop. He then glanced at his watch and said, 'Oh yes, you are right.'

Mirko heaved a sigh of relief and said in fluent and crisp French, 'My fiancée is waiting for me at the top of the hill. I have to reach her before the bar closes.'

'What is your fiancée doing in a bar at the top of a hill?'

'Lamenting for me, of course. What else?' Mirko said and then added, 'But she is not as beautiful as you are. She would be green with envy if she were to see you.'

'No way!' Yohan cut in. 'She won't be able to see Bipasha. Bipasha is leaving very early tomorrow.'

'But before that Bipasha will meet Yanka.' Mirko said in a calm voice. 'I am now going to take Bipasha to the hilltop. One of you is welcome to come along. As you well know, my car can accommodate at the most four people. That too, quite tightly packed.'

Yohan laughed and said, 'Who are you to whisk away my guest? I will come along to guard her. This is not the land of the lumpen proletariat, mister. You might be a very celebrated playwright, but in this country you cannot have fun with two ladies by your side.'

'Playwright? Me?' Mirko gazed at him with pure amazement in his eyes. 'I am a mechanic, I work in a garage. Bipasha dear, did you take me to be a playwright? My apologies. These intellectual communists can lie left, right and, centre. I am a labourer…I work hard to earn my living. These people are intellectuals, they work for the university. And Gjorge, he is a great poet. I am a mere factory worker…a true proletariat. The true face of Czechoslovakia. Or, you can say, the real Slovakia. This southern country of Slovakia is the land of the poor communists. And the northern state of the Czechs, home of the bright city of Prague, is the land of the rich communists.'

'Mirko!' Again everyone scolded him in unison. 'You are leading Bipasha into an impossible maze. What opinion do you think she is forming of this country?'

'I am setting the stage so that she can think what she ought to think…' Mirko smiled a little and placed his hand on Bipasha's bare waist. 'Come on beautiful, let me take you to the top of the hill. If you want, I can show you my factory on the way. Though this envious devil, Yohan, will also be with us. Anyway, not that we have an option. In socialist countries, it is the duty of a citizen to sacrifice personal pleasure for the welfare of society! We will have to bear with Yohan's unwanted company.'

# THREE

Mirko drove his new, plastic-bodied, little white car very carefully along the circuitous hill roads. There were few cars on the road and Bipasha learnt that most were made in Russia.

Once on the hilltop, Mirko said, 'Look, there lies Slovakia and its people beneath our feet. This looking downwards is what your imperfect colonialism teaches you to do. Isn't it? Of course, the university people exercise an apolitical approach and employ this attitude in all spheres. Isn't that so, Yohan?'

Yohan did not reply. Perhaps, he had decided not to participate in any more arguments. Bipasha had noticed that even while fighting, they had not slowed down on their drinking.

There was no way Bipasha could leave her coat in the car. The moment she alighted, the extreme cold chilled her to the bones. Below them Slovakia lay scattered like a throw of countless coloured dots of light.

Mirko said, 'Just a moment, let me find out when Yanka finishes work.'

Bipasha and Yohan climbed back into the car, which was parked in the middle of a garden. In front of them was a white bungalow, which housed a restaurant. From within, floated out, foot-tapping strains of modern music.

A little later, Mirko returned with a very peculiar looking girl. Her hair was silver coloured and, at first glance, she looked like an octogenarian lady. But then, it became evident that she had coloured her hair to get the look of a platinum-blonde. Yanka's nails and lips were also painted in silver. She wore a pink micro-mini skirt and a white top with a lace apron tied around her waist. A small lace cap was perched on her head. Her legs were long and well-shaped. Her eyes were naturally deep-set, though her bosom was just the opposite. Yanka could be anything between twenty-six and fifty-six.

Yanka was very pleased to see them. She smiled widely, revealing white teeth and sending a ripple over the skin of her gaunt face. Then she led them inside and took their coats away.

Bipasha's jaw dropped as she entered the room. In these few days, she had concluded that the Czechoslovakian way of life was very dull, lifeless and gloomy; almost bordering on unhappiness. Her enquiry had revealed that Danish lived in a two-room hostel with his wife and two children. Evichka lived in a similar one-room hostel with her husband. None of them had a kitchen and they usually ate out. They also shared common bathrooms. What kind of a life was this? The streets were dimly lit. And as for the bars and restaurants, one had to peep inside to find out if they were open for business. This was the first time she heard blaring music and loud voices ruling the scene. Yanka seated them in a corner of the room that was separated from the main area by a curtain of beads, hanging from a thin wooden frame.

The open area was what attracted attention. A group of young boys—students, according to Yohan—were dancing on table tops and singing to the strains of a guitar-like stringed instrument. A few girls too, sat around the tables, but they were not participants of the wild musical show. Another waitress, dressed like Yanka, went up to the boys from time to time and put in some sort of a request. But the unruly bunch paid no heed.

Soon, a male waiter walked up to the boys, and a bellowing reprimand could be heard over the music and singing. Yet, the show went on. In the meanwhile, Yanka had served them a carafe of red wine with three glasses. She though, did not join them. Yohan interpreted her refusal, 'We are not allowed to drink when on duty.'

Since Bipasha had bid farewell to Gjorge, Danish, and Evichka, Yohan had been acting as her interpreter. Bechka though, was still in service. She would fetch Bipasha from her hostel tomorrow around five in the morning and take her to the city. Danish and Evichka had taken their leave with warm kisses on both her cheeks. But Gjorge's handshake had been cool and hard. Bipasha did not like it at all. From time to time, Bipasha thought of Danish and Eva; quite possibly, she would never see them again. In fact, that would be quite natural and expected. Was there a twinge in her heart? Mirko was talking to Yanka. From their looks, Bipasha could make out that they were discussing her. Yohan sat relaxed, his hand stretched along the back of Bipasha's chair, smelling of sweat and wine.

Yohan said, 'It's time for the bar to close, but the boys are not letting them close...drunk as they are.

They are singing away…one folksong after another. Actually, they sing quite well.'

Yanka appeared quite flustered, as she could not sit with them for long. She had to attend to the dinner guests at the tables she served and tried her best to squeeze out time to come and sit with them every now and then.

At the table adjacent to theirs, sat a corpulent middle-aged couple. The lady's puffed up hair had been coloured black, her lips painted red, her eyelids shaded blue, her chubby cheeks tinged in pink, and so on. She wore a formal evening gown in black and a fresh rose rested happily on her well-displayed bosom. The gentleman too, appeared nicely groomed in his black suit and fair bald pate.

At another table, a seasoned violinist serenaded a young couple, who appeared quite pleased by the attention.

As soon as the violinist drew on the last chord, the rotund gentleman from the next table summoned him to his table. The musician obliged and, taking up position close to them, he pushed his instrument into service, piercing the air with strong renditions of musical notes. The lady's face was immediately wreathed in an ear-to-ear grin of overflowing delight.

Yanka asked Mirko—would he like to engage the musician for Bipasha's pleasure? Though Bipasha did not understand the language, she could very well make out the intention and immediately lodged an objection. Yohan came to her rescue, 'Mirko, the bar is about to close. Please don't create any issues now.'

This was something Yanka could not refute. In the meanwhile, the wild dancing and singing at the other table had come to a grinding halt, and the boys were settling their bills, albeit much grudgingly. The girls too, appeared ready to leave.

The violinist continued to play a romantic tune, close to the plump lady's ears. Yanka finished a round of her tables; it was now time for everyone to call it a day. Soon, as was the custom in restaurants in this part of the world, the lights were dimmed. Gradually, they were switched off, and a lone light remained in service to show them the way out, through the maze of chairs and tables.

After leaving the restaurant, they again piled into the car. This time, Bipasha sat in the rear seat with Yohan while Yanka sat beside Mirko in the front. Yanka had changed into a floral-print dress with a bright red coat on top, and tied her hair back with a ribbon. Out of her uniform of pink skirt, white apron, and white cap, Yanka looked younger. Clearly on the right side of thirty; yet, she and Mirko did not make a well-matched pair. This girl would not be able to share Mirko's dreams, she did not know how to dream. Nevertheless, they were all set to wed in the coming summer. Mirko had noted down Bipasha's address, while at the restaurant, so that they could send her an invite.

Yanka had a kind of steeliness about her. She looked like a girl who earned her living through hard work. In the past, she was a factory worker, like her parents. Presently, she worked as a barmaid and lived in a working girls' hostel. And, Bipasha was surprised to hear, she spent her weekends with Mirko.

Only Bechka, a farmer's daughter, lived with her parents on their farm, and that is where she returned to from Yohan's office. Her parents would be waiting up for her, so she must return home at night.

The difference between Yanka and Bechka was quite stark, Bipasha felt. Yanka was a city girl and a labourer. Her rough and tanned face told the story of a family that led a smoke-soot-smeared life of hard labour in factories. While Bechka's mellow beauty, her glowing health, and her bashful nature told the tale of a life spent in the fresh air amidst fresh farm produce. They appeared about the same age—around twenty-five, perhaps a year or two apart.

There still seemed to be quite a gap between city and village ways of life, between labourers and farmers. This should have become a thing of the past—a romantic, theoretical difference only. Bipasha had not expected to find such a glaring difference still existing between the two stereotypes of factory labourers and farmers. Although it did exist in India and in the US, the two extreme instances of economy. But here? In this socialist state, too?

How surprising! Did no one live in a 'home'? None of those Bipasha had met so far, lived in family quarters. She was yet to be introduced to a 'proper' couple. She had not come across a baby or an incapable old person. She had not seen a kitchen or a bedroom. Could she really say that she had 'seen' this country? All she visited were universities, museum exhibitions, and restaurants. What kind of state hospitality was this?

'How sad! I was hardly able to see your country!' She grumbled.

'What! Why?' A shiver ran down Yohan. As it was, they sat squashed against each other in the meagre confines of the car. Yohan's knees jutted upwards and almost touched his chin. Bipasha's petite frame saved her a similar predicament. Yohan sat resting his long arm along Bipasha's back, and gradually that warm and curious hand sat heavier and heavier on her shoulders, like the collective responsibilities of the world.

'Why do you say that?' The shiver that ran down Yohan now made its way into Bipasha due to the inescapable physical proximity.

'You haven't seen my country!' Yohan exclaimed and squeezed Bipasha's shoulder in a brotherly fashion. 'What a disaster! Tell me, what would you like to see? We still have about five hours in hand, right?'

'Why do you have to leave tomorrow? Stay back for another couple of days.' Mirko said in French.

Yanka did not know French and immediately asked him to interpret. Bipasha had noticed that when Yohan said something in French or English, Yanka did not bother with an explanation but when Mirko said something in an unfamiliar language, she demanded an interpretation. Mirko always explained everything to her patiently and with affection.

Now Mirko spoke to Yanka and then said, 'Yanka is also of the same mind. Bipasha should not leave now…the weekend is just beginning.'

Yohan though, appeared quite serious as he said, 'What has happened, Bipasha? Why did you say that?'

Bipasha felt slightly discomfited, but still she said, 'In these few days, I have not met a single family. What kind of a country is this? Why do you live in hostels? Well, if it was a commune then this would have made sense. I can even understand the concept of kibbutz. But that is not the case here. What kind of a life do you lead?'

Mirko broke into a deafening laugh, 'Oh dear, this is just a coincidence! Everyone lives with their respective families. Only some students, although married, live in hostels to cope with tight finances. The moment their finances improve they set up home together. Eva and Danish are still students. As for me, I am still a wayward wanderer. But Gjorge lives in his own home, though alone. And that is one place I am not going to send you to! Elizabeth does not live in the city. You could have easily gone with her today and found out what a farm is like.'

'How could I go uninvited? She did not ask me, did she?'

'How could she? No one can express their desires in fear of Yohan. I happen to be quite an animal, so managed to have my way and bring you here. Do you think Yohan is happy about it?' Mirko intervened.

'You are right, I am not at all happy. You are a gorilla!' Yohan groused.

Suddenly Mirko said, 'Here is your solution, Bipasha. There, in front of us, is one of Yohan's homes. Yohan has three flats—one in Bratislava, one here, and the other in his office...the one you visited. There he has arrangements to spend the night. A complete set of bedding is stored inside the big divan. How many homes would you like to see? Help yourself! He even has a wife, two children, and a mother...our professor is an established family man. If you visit his home, you will know all about the lifestyle of the rich in Czechoslovakia.'

As Mirko was talking, he drove into a courtyard. Two tall buildings were on either side and, in each, a well-lit staircase rising to the twelfth floor could be seen through glass windows. Witness and company to some sleepless inhabitants, light shone through a few windows here and there. Surprisingly though, it wasn't even one in the morning, and the neighbourhood was already steeped in the silence of slumber.

'Would you like to go in? Have a look at how the professors live? Get an idea of their standard of living!

Your girls' hostel is just about a ten-minute walk from here.'

Bipasha looked at Yohan, query in her eyes. But Yohan was gazing at the building in a very preoccupied manner, quite lost in thought.

'Yohan, will you walk her to the hostel after showing her your home? Or should we all come in? Won't it be unfair on the sleeping family, if we all were to troop in so late?'

'But their sleep will be disturbed anyway, even if one person went in,' Bipasha argued.

'Oh no! Yohan's wife is an extremely fashionable and arrogant lady. After all, she is a Hungarian countess! She does not deem fit to recognise Slovaks, like us, as humans. But, am sure, she will know you as one of her own kind. Look at the amount of gold you have on you!'

Gold? Of course! For the first time, Bipasha realised how many items of gold jewellery she wore—bangles, earrings, a chain around her neck. Surprisingly, all these were part of regular wear for most middle-class Bengali women. There was even a ring on her finger and her saree was studded with golden flowers. Truly, she was laden with gold! Samir, you made me take these off, but I have put them back on. Samir, I have picked up all the discarded pieces. All of them.

Yohan abruptly flung open the car door and got out. Then he offered Bipasha his right hand and said, 'Very well, come on. I'll see you to the hostel by half past one. You have to leave early in the morning.'

'That's more like it!' Mirko applauded. As Yanka hugged and kissed her goodbye, the strong smell of cheap cosmetic products raged an assault on Bipasha's nostrils.

Mirko said, 'Why should Yanka be the only one to kiss you? I will too.' And before the words could even sink into her, Bipasha was trapped in an iron-hard, military-like embrace, with her cheeks received smacking, tingling kisses as parting presents.

As they drove off, Mirko stuck his head out into the rain through his window and shouted, 'Write to me! Don't forget this Mirko, Bipasha…do write, our little green grasshopper! And take the tulip back with you. It will remind you of Mirko through the entire season of spring. I'll never forget you, grasshopper… never…'

◄○►

# FOUR

—•◆•—

*Jamais je ne t'oublirais*—along with these lines from a song Mirko was singing, the little white plastic car gradually disappeared into the dim haze of the road.

Yohan wrapped a protective arm around the tulip-hugging Bipasha and ran to the portico to escape the rain. The portico though, was not much, surely nothing like the usual sprawling porches; it was a tiny, shaded area, like the ones one would find near a gate. Yohan fished out a chunky bunch of keys from his pocket and unlocked the main door; then he quickly pushed Bipasha inside. Bipasha waited in front of the lift as Yohan shut the door gently; careful not to make any noise. Then he whispered, 'Don't talk. It is quite late.'

After pressing the lift's call button for what seemed like ages, Yohan said in a disgusted voice, 'Am sure they have not shut the collapsible door of the lift properly. Rubbish!'

Bipasha felt quite amused. This too, was so much like the ways of her countrymen. People from the West would never make this mistake. After all, the capitalists had to look after their own interests. In a socialist state, such mistakes seemed possible.

Bipasha had never had the revolutionary streak in her. It was through Samir that she got into revolution, not the other way round...she did not get Samir through revolution. This was where the big difference lay between a true revolutionary and Bipasha. Bipasha could not see her revolutionary act to the end; ultimately, she had to surrender to her father and her brothers. Accepting the forceful ways of her father as her destiny, she escaped to England. It was five years now that she left her country, and she had not been able to muster the guts to go back.

On the one hand was the political party, and on the other was the police department, not to say of Samir, in prison; who could Bipasha face and how? Bipasha had already conceded defeat in front of all the weaknesses that middle-class Indian girls usually faced and tried to fight.

Samir had never used the lift in their building on Park Street where they had a flat. He always preferred to take the stairs to the third floor. Those buildings were luxurious ones, belonging to the Raj era, at the most five or six storied, not like the ten or twelve storied modern ones.

Samir, I don't know how to convince you that my father compelled me to go to Mumbai. I did not leave you of my own will, Samir.

The lift did not come down.

'You wait here. I'll go up and bring the lift down. Give me the flowers,' Yohan said. Snatching the tub out of her hands, he started to run up the stairs. Bipasha decided otherwise and followed. Yohan looked back at her and gestured her to keep quiet and tiptoe up.

Bipasha was quite amused. A celebrated professor, who featured in the elite list of world renowned literary critics, was tiptoeing to his own home lest he disturbed the neighbours. What consideration! Just as there were some who did not shut the lift door, there were also people like Yohan.

Bipasha did not count how many flights they ascended. She blindly followed the figure in front of her in a heavy black coat, dirty blue jeans, a briefcase tucked under an arm, and a tub with a flowering tulip plant held tightly. Yohan tackled the stairs two or three in one leap, his tennis shoes making no sound at all.

Climbing at the heels of that gigantic frame was tiny Bipasha, who kept pace but not in leaps and bounds. Her stilettos were bound to make sharp tick-tack sounds, so she had taken them off and was carrying the pair in her hand. She too, made no sound as she climbed the stairs softly in her stocking-clad feet.

Yohan stopped in front of a flat on their right. He then transferred the flower tub to his side and turned towards Bipasha, placing a finger over his lips, 'Shh!'

Thinking that she perhaps looked smaller without her heels on, Bipasha felt kind of embarrassed. She longed to enter the flat and climb back into the stilettos. She took a few steps and relieved Yohan of the tulips.

Yohan was again shuffling through his bunch of keys trying to find the right one. Finally, luck favoured and he unlocked the door, holding it open for Bipasha to enter. Bipasha walked in and found herself in a dark corridor. She had noticed a similar door on the left side of the staircase. But that corridor had a light on. Why was this dark?

Yohan followed her in and then slowly shut the heavy glass door that clicked close on a brass self-lock. Then started another round of Yohan's usual game of find-the-right-key to open another door at the other end of the dark corridor. His clumsiness amazed

Bipasha. Was this the way someone entered his own home? It was more like sneaking into someone else's flat. Yohan was looking through the keys in the light coming in through the glass door from the staircase. He clutched the bag of keys tightly so that the jingle of the keys did not prove to be hazardous to the treasured slumber of his esteemed neighbours. And, from time to time, he put a finger to his lips to remind Bipasha to keep her vocal chords in check.

Bipasha smiled at Yohan's antics. Gosh! Felt like they were on a secret rendezvous to enjoy the fruits of an illegitimate relationship. A much married man was taking a foreign guest to his home to show her the lifestyle of a Czechoslovakian family. What was all the hush-hush about? Why such secrecy? Where was the need to behave like conspirators?

Yohan was quite strange in his ways. In the presence of others, he wasted no time in falling all over her to express his liking. And now, when they were alone, he was almost comatose in fear! Why was he so scared? At worst, his neighbours would wake up... that's it. Come to think of it, how would they wake up? Any sound to break through the glass doors and reach the bedrooms of the neighbours was impossible.

Bipasha often thought that these European nations had not been able to free themselves of the secretive and conspiratorial atmosphere, which had existed during the rule of Stalin. They feared for no reason. Inside the car, the rolled up windows, their warm breaths and the forced physical proximity had created a feeling of intimacy between them. Yohan's fearful and anxious behaviour shattered that. Something seemed amiss to Bipasha and the dark corridor kind of overwhelmed her. Soon, Yohan pulled her into the room and shut the door softly.

What kind of darkness was this? She could see nothing, hear nothing. The fresh yet strong smell of this new unfamiliar colour of darkness entered her lungs. Bipasha inhaled deeply, not only the air but some of the dark night as well. An unknown feeling, hanging between anticipation and apprehension, took over her senses.

How strange! Where was Yohan? And why weren't the lights on? Why was a single light not left on in the flat when the master of the set-up was out? Hanging on to the flower tub with one hand, Bipasha groped with the other in search of a switch. Thinking that usually there would be a switch by the door, she felt in that area and found one. Aha! Now she would be able to shed light on the goings on. She worked the switch with a trembling hand.

No light.

'Yohan!' In the still darkness, her low voice sounded like a scream.

'Yes, darling.' The reply came from someplace very close by.

'Light? Won't the lights come on?' Bipasha implored in a petrified voice.

'No, darling,' Yohan replied and switched on his lighter instead with one hand. In the light of that, Bipasha noticed him holding a thick half-melted candle, stuck on a saucer.

Lighting the candle, Yohan laughed; his features too, appeared more relaxed. He then put the candle down on the floor and, taking the flower tub from Bipasha, deposited that beside it. Then he proceeded to relieve Bipasha of her coat very politely.

'The electricity connection has been severed because the bill was not cleared!' He explained and laughed softly. He hung up Bipasha's coat inside a nearby wardrobe, and then took off his own coat.

The top buttons of his green shirt were still undone, and the golden hair on his chest, visible through the gaping shirt front, appeared quite animalistic. A shiver ran down Bipasha. But, immediately, she suppressed the feeling and reprimanded herself—are you an animal that your senses sprang to life at the sight of bare flesh in candlelight?

Aloud she said, 'What! They have really cut your connection because you didn't pay the bill? Don't they give you a warning?'

'They did. But I was not here.'

'How strange! But your wife is here…is she living in this darkness with the children?'

Yohan did not reply. Instead, he smiled a little and, closing the wardrobe doors, took off his shoes and socks and slipped into a pair of silken slippers. He then offered Bipasha a similar pair of red slippers and said, 'Put these on. You'll feel comfortable.'

Bipasha was not keen to slip into someone else's shoes and said, 'No, I am fine. I like walking barefoot.'

'You won't like it. The heater will not be on.'

'But it's not cold. Some heat must be coming from the central heating system.'

'Not really.'

'Then why am I not feeling cold?'

'Perhaps the credit goes to your youth. Or mine?' Yohan's gaze flooded Bipasha with a certain heat.

She again reprimanded herself. What are you doing, Bipasha? What's wrong with you?

Then she whispered, 'I would say it's more your wife's credit. She is sleeping, isn't she?'

Yohan held up the candle and said, 'Let's go inside.' Then he grabbed Bipasha's hand and strode ahead. As she followed Yohan, Bipasha felt like counting the footsteps…a niggling uneasiness fluttered inside her.

…five, six, seven, eight…

'This is our living room.'

In the candlelight, Bipasha saw a medium-sized room, which was starkly bare. In one corner there was a small teapoy on which stood a used glass tumbler. On one wall hung a furry stretch of material, possibly the hide of some animal. And on another wall was a wide window, over which a pair of brown canvas curtains had been drawn close. There was nothing else in the room except for the inexpensive rug, which covered the floor. Was this the living room? Where did people sit? What about sofa, chairs, tables, furniture?

'Isn't that wall-hanging nice?' Yohan asked, pointing to the furry hide. 'I quite like it. Got it from Yugoslavia.'

Bipasha was quite stunned by Yohan's easy-going attitude; as though this bare room with only a wall-hanging to sit proxy for furniture was an absolutely normal occurrence! It reminded Bipasha of the famous painting, 'Olympia', where the reclining nude female's nudity is made all the more prominent by her stiletto-clad feet.

Bipasha couldn't stop herself from saying, 'Instead of hanging it on the wall had you spread it on the floor people could have at least sat on it.'

'Oh dear! How can such a nice thing be used to sit on? People are free to sit wherever else they please.'

'But where?'

Bipasha had never come to terms with this European liking for animal skins. To her, it portrayed a kind of barbarism, a sort of caveman-like primitive taste. But, as she had found, displaying animal skins as wall-hangings and bedspreads, and using them for other decorative purposes happened to indicate elite taste among Europeans! In East Europe, she had found them mainly flaunted as wall-hangings. Women often wrapped fox and mink furs as scarves around their necks and wore coats made out of cheetah skins. Bipasha found this trend to be quite vulgar and graceless; bordering on cruelty and in very bad taste, hinting at uncivilised mentality.

What suited the ash-smeared, matted-haired Lord Shiva was sure to be a glaring misfit on ladies with polished nails and painted faces! The display of strength that was established through the possession of animal skins represented nothing but a decadent civilisation.

These new socialist states should not be home to such things. Bipasha's thoughts ran along these lines but she changed the topic, 'Won't you wake up your wife? Would have loved to see your children too but don't want to spoil their sleep.'

The shadows flung on the walls by the flickering candle flame filled up the empty room. A deprived and bare room, whose only adornment was a dead animal's skin.

Bipasha did not like it at all. It felt like a cave to her. She quickly steered the conversation to the subject of children—the way people launch into divine chants to ward off evil spirits. Children were the world's purest, and Bipasha hoped her attempt would take the conversation away from the gruesome association to animal skins.

'It is hard to really know a country unless one meets its young and old.'

Yohan walked out of the room without replying and Bipasha followed.

Entering the next room, Yohan held the candle aloft. There was a big and bright poster on the wall in red, blue, and yellow. It showed soldiers marching with their fists raised high; Bipasha could not make head or tail of the writing though the word 'Czechoslovakia' did stand out. It was a small room; on one wall was the poster, and against another wall stood a bunk bed, quite like those found in military camps. The two-tiered bed had mattresses but no sheets.

'This is my children's room.'

'But where are they? The beds are empty!'

'They are not here.'

'Are they away for the weekend?' Bipasha looked at the bed and wondered about the absence of bed sheets, pillows, and blankets. The mattresses lay bare, almost naked.

'No, not for the weekend. They are away visiting their maternal grandparents in Hungary.'

'Alone?'

'No, with their mother.'

'What do you mean? Isn't your wife home?'

'My wife doesn't like living in Czechoslovakia.'

'You can't mean Hungary is a better place than Czechoslovakia? Even after 1956?'

'Shush! Sometimes you talk without thinking, Bipasha! Don't say such things here...even walls have ears! Actually, Hungary has the advantage of a big city like Budapest. My wife belongs to that big city. She has her own cultural life there. In this little town of Nitra, she feels suffocated.'

'Why don't you live in Bratislava?'

'That too doesn't have much. Yes, if you were to talk about Prague, I would say that is a proper big city. But I cannot work out of Prague.'

'Yohan, before bringing me, why didn't you tell me your wife is not here?'

'Did Mirko give me a chance?'

'I gathered Mirko is not too fond of your wife... he did make a dig at her title.'

'Mirko is not very wrong. He is crazy and often blurts out the truth without thinking through. And that is the problem with Mirko.'

'Why didn't you tell him that your wife is in Hungary? Where is the problem?'

'Why don't you try and solve that puzzle?'

'I can't think of anything.'

'Come...let me first show you the other rooms.' Yohan took Bipasha's hand and led her out of the room. But, surprisingly, something seem to have changed. Bipasha's hand felt damp, and she wanted to pull it away. But she didn't…rather, couldn't. Her hand seemed to be glued to his by some unknown lure.

'Yohan.'

'Yes, darling?'

'Doesn't your mother live here as well?'

'Yes, she does. And the room I am about to show you is hers.'

Yohan opened the door to another room. This room had a bed covered in a heavy red bedspread. No pillows were in sight…of course, in Czechoslovakia, pillows and blankets were stored in a cleverly fitted drawer by the side of the bed. Beds were always neat and tidy! The walls were bare, but there was a table and a chair. There were some papers in a tray on the table. For a change, this room had the feel of being lived in though, presently, there was no sign of any inhabitant.

'Where is your mother?'

'She has gone to Prague. She works in the education department and travels often.'

'You mean, there is no one at home?' Bipasha's voice sounded hollow, like the wind blowing over the dark fields at night.

'Are you afraid, Bipasha?' Yohan brought his arm around to encircle Bipasha's shoulder. And, immediately, a stifled shiver shot down Bipasha's body right to the tips of her toes.

'I wanted to see a complete family home, not a vacant house,' Bipasha said.

'That is why I didn't invite you here. I didn't want to cheat you. But the situation, back then, reached a point of no return.'

'Why? You could have easily told Mirko that no one was home. They would have dropped me at the hostel. And now, you will have to go out in the rain for no reason, just for me.'

'That's nothing. Much more important to me is the fact that you have graced this vacant home of mine with your presence, you have filled it up with your fragrance. But it has been selfish of me to have dragged you to this empty flat in this rainy weather. Now you will have to walk in the rain, and you have a long journey ahead of you tomorrow. In fact, you have every right to be angry with me.'

As he spoke, Yohan pulled Bipasha closer for a few moments with the hand that rested around her shoulders. In his other hand, he still held the candle.

The room they walked into next, was filled with various household items. Most were still in cardboard boxes, yet to be unpacked. Some other things lay strewn haphazardly.

'Here, look! This is my home!' Clothes, shoes, books, and utensils appeared to spill over the sides of the boxes. What a strange man Yohan was!

'This is our master bedroom. It belongs to me and my countess wife. Do you understand?'

The room was nothing better than a store. One wall was covered by canvas curtains, and Bipasha learnt that there was a long window along the entire stretch of that wall—what they called a picture window. The curtains were similar to those in the living room.

'I am sure this is temporary. These curtains will have to go, right?'

'Why?' Yohan asked, surprised.

Bipasha gazed intently at the dull brown canvas curtains. She recalled the heavy and expensive curtains she had seen at the restaurant and also the tapestry-type satin curtains in Yohan's office.

Yohan realised what she meant, and said, 'These will stay, and there will also be some fancy curtains beneath. That is my mother's department, I don't bother with it.'

'Mother? Doesn't your wife look into these things?'

'She has done up the flat in Bratislava. You would be stunned by the décor...It is in the bourgeois style…rather, the feudal style, I should say. She brought over many of her personal possessions and decorated the flat with those. I feel quite embarrassed actually. But my wife refuses to understand. This is my mother's flat. She is not a countess…she is a school teacher. This is a proletariat's flat.'

'Will you show me a photo of your mother?'

'Photo? Why…all of a sudden?'

'Just like that. Aren't there photos of your wife and children here?'

'Sure…in the albums. But I'm not sure in which box the albums are…'

Bipasha looked around at the countless boxes; some gaping open, some closed. The place looked like a railway-station platform where a goods train had been offloaded. She then raised her face and looked at Yohan.

Yohan said, 'Wait a minute. There might be a couple of photos here…' Saying that, he knelt on the floor and started to rummage through a kind of box-file.

And, voila! Not a couple but three or four photos, that too in colour. An arrogant beauty, of around thirty-five, posed with two extremely haughty looking little boys. They stood ramrod straight, in military fashion, with tight smiles on their lips. In a second photo, a silver-haired elderly lady stood in a group of people.

Yohan pointed to it and said, 'My mother with her colleagues.'

Bipasha liked the look of his mother. In another, the arrogant lady posed with two people, all of them looking relaxed and laughing. But wait...what was that in the background? Wasn't it the lotus-shaped window of Notre Dame?

Bipasha said, 'Hey, this is exactly like Notre Dame. Is there a replica in Czechoslovakia?'

'That is Notre Dame.'

'Was your wife visiting Paris?'

'She is visiting...she is now in Paris. Of course, this photo is from last year. That is a nephew of hers who lives in Paris.'

'Paris? But didn't you say they were in Hungary?'

'Bipasha, please don't ask me any more questions. Please...I am telling you the truth. Only the truth. But please don't share any of this with Bechka when you see her tomorrow. This is a deep secret, a very important secret for me.'

'Why? Is visiting Paris prohibited?'

'You won't understand. There is nothing prohibited as such...yet, there is a lot that is not acceptable. My wife is not on a short visit to Paris. She went to Hungary and then fled to Paris from there.'

'Fled? What do you mean?'

'I'll tell you everything, Bipasha. My darling… my sweet little Bipasha…Mirko has rightly called you a green grasshopper. I'll tell you…but not now…is that alright? We'll talk about it later.'

Fear coursed through Bipasha as Yohan took her in his arms. He had already relieved himself of the candle when he was looking for the photos. They were both kneeling on the floor searching for photos. Now Yohan had suddenly and swiftly laid her back on the floor. Yohan's shirt hung open, and Bipasha could smell his bare chest, which hovered very close to her.

A warning bell rang in Bipasha's head, and her mind sprang to action in preparation of something… she did not know what. It seemed as though someone had activated a very important signal for her benefit And it was time for the train to arrive. The bell rang and rang…were she to press her ears to the railway track, she would have heard the sound of the approaching train….

Samir, come and take a look. Look at the condition of what you once considered your sole property.

Samir used to say, 'I am a capitalist regarding one thing. That is you. You are my property…my private property.'

Caressing her in their most intimate moments, Samir would say, 'It is for this girl that I will never become a pure communist.'

Samir, I was not fit for you. I am a flighty grasshopper, like Mirko said. Look at my infidelity. Look how my unfaithful body is responding…how my warm blood is dancing along as they course through my veins; just the way it used to when you touched me. Look, Samir…the body is a wild animal… it cannot be tamed…it belongs to whichever jungle it passes through.

Bipasha forcefully pulled herself up as she was about to sink into a soft and languid state. Yohan's lips were too near, and she used all her might to push against his chest. Please let him pull away…it was time he pulled away.

'I am thirsty, Yohan. Oh! It's so hot in here.'

Yohan released Bipasha and got to his feet. Then he offered his right hand to pull her up. But Bipasha stood up by herself.

Bipasha bent low to pick up the candle but, perhaps, to the sudden flapping of her saree, the candle went out. Again, time began to sink into a dense darkness, with Bipasha and Yohan in its fold.

Bipasha cried out, 'Yohan?'

'I'm here, darling.' The lighter sprang into flame. 'Give me the candle.'

Yohan lit the candle and walked away with it, murmuring to himself, 'Wonder what drinks are in stock…if there are any, at all. After all, this is not a home!'

'Just plain water will do. Is that available?' Bipasha asked nervously.

'Of course. Why won't we have water when there is a bathroom and a kitchen?'

'Well…I wondered if the connection to that had also been severed. I am quite confused about the ways of your socialist state.'

'Oh come on, you crazy girl! Even in capitalist states they cut off the electricity connection, if you fail to pay the bill. Why, don't they do the same in your country?'

'Surely that must be the law. But I don't know if they actually do it.'

'How will you know? You are from a wealthy family.'

'How did you know? From my attire? Well, that hardly tells you anything.'

'This is our kitchen.' The room was longish. Along one wall was a small square table with two chairs. On the table, besides a salt-and-pepper stand, was a narrow-necked glass vase, holding plastic flowers. Bipasha was a trifle surprised at first but then instantly recalled Yohan's words—after all, this was not a home. Along the opposite wall was a sink with twin taps, a medium-size fridge, and a cooking hob. Bipasha turned on the tap and held her hand under it. Cold water...aah!

'Here...' Yohan held out a glass tumbler. Bipasha felt quite soothed after a drink. Then she turned on the other tap and soon hot water flowed.

'Didn't you say there is no electricity?'

'That is a separate connection. There is hot water in the bathroom as well. I am going to take a shower. Would you like one?'

'Shower! Why?'

'Just like that...if you want to. The bathroom is on the other side of this wall.' Yohan said and pointed towards that side.

With much curiosity, Bipasha set off in that direction. There was a small toilet with a separate door and a small bathroom with a peculiar looking big round tub on the floor with two taps and a shower head. Bipasha guessed it was the bathtub. There was a heavy plastic curtain, which could be drawn around it while bathing. There was also a big round bath soap, a large white and yellow towel, and a bath mat on the floor.

'Did you take a tour of the bathroom?' Yohan asked. 'Would you like a shower to test it out?'

'Oh no. Why would I want to take a shower at someone else's place?'

Suddenly, Yohan laughed out loudly. 'Why? Don't people use the toilet at other people's houses? If that is okay then where is the harm in taking a shower?' Having said that, he abruptly stopped laughing and said, 'Gosh! I think I laughed out a bit too loudly. The way you behave makes me laugh!'

'What's wrong in laughing loudly? Your neighbours must laugh too! Where's the problem? I don't like this hushed up atmosphere at all.'

That was all Bipasha had been experiencing since she had entered the flat. It had started with her having to take off her stilettos lest they made any noise. Then, after entering the flat, she had spoken in whispers so as not to wake up the children. But now, when it had been established that there wasn't a third soul in the flat, where was the need to whisper?

'Yohan, you are too obsessed with your neighbours. People live with neighbours everywhere in the world.'

The candle had almost burnt itself out. Yohan stretched out his hand and reached for something on a high shelf behind the fridge. It turned out to be a fresh candle, and he lit the new one from the old. Again light flooded around them.

'How romantic!' Yohan chuckled and winked at her. Then he set the candle down on the table and said, 'A candlelight evening for two. And that is where the problem lies! If the neighbours find out that I brought you to this flat then…'

'Really?'

'Our socialist state is kind of prudish when it comes to sexual morality.'

'What do you mean? Isn't that petty bourgeois mentality? Minds groomed along the norms of a socialist state should not be thinking that way.'

'Well, no one really knows what should and what should not be happening. All we know is what is happening at this moment. Here, scandal spreads like wildfire and has the power to cause much harm. I hold a responsible position in this chapter of the party. Hence I have to tread very carefully.'

As he spoke, Yohan unscrewed the cap of a narrow-necked bottle and poured out a spoonful of the thick liquid into a glass. Then he held the glass under the tap and topped it up with cold water. He offered Bipasha the glass saying, 'Sorry, don't have ice. But the water is cold.'

'What is this?' Bipasha looked at the yellowish drink in her hand.

'Made you a glass of orange juice from concentrate. There is no other drink in here...neither hard nor soft. The fridge, too, is empty.'

The mention of 'orange concentrate' almost chased away whatever desire Bipasha may have had towards drinking the same. She was sure that it would taste like medicine. She took a hesitant sip. No...not bad. Almost like fresh orange juice.

'Won't you have some?'

'Juices and soft drinks are not for me. I am a hardliner. You get that, little girl?'

'Yes, I do. But am I to drink alone then?'

'Well, you can share yours with me...' Yohan picked up the glass from the table and took a sip from it. And, immediately, revulsion surged up within Bipasha. This was another behaviour she had not come to terms with. It seemed, there was much of the West that this Indo-Anglian poet, Bipasha Chowdhury, was yet to embrace.

Samir, I am not as posh as you always believed me to be. My knowledge of Bengali may have been thrown into slight disarray because I went to an English-medium convent school, but my values were never at threat; they have remained intact. This half-and-half Bipasha disliked sharing crockery and cutlery. Yet, many a time, I have drunk tea from your cup. Why didn't I feel this revulsion then? Samir, why didn't I shy away from sharing a cup with you? You were a scrawny, poor boy, who went to a Bengali-medium school in suburban Kolkata; who had grown up wearing washed-till-threadbare cheap shirts and dirty pyjamas. You may have bagged a scholarship, and you may have been a popular figure in Presidency College but, nevertheless, your meagre background can hardly be denied. So, why didn't I feel disgusted? Yet, with Yohan...

'Enjoy your drink while I take a quick shower.' Yohan yanked away his shirt, baring his body, as he said this.

Bipasha's head buzzed and warmth engulfed her ears, as though someone had abruptly slapped her hard. The phrase 'crude sex appeal' was usually used with reference to women and with respect to men in Hollywood movies occasionally. But now, all of a sudden, the reality of it flashed clear in front of Bipasha. Not the Victor Mature or John Wayne kind; Yohan's muscular and perfectly toned physique appeared to be a storehouse of extreme power, like a bolt of lightning. He could easily release it, if he so wished. Or create an explosion even. At other times, Yohan's preoccupied demeanour and his dishevelled attire camouflaged this quite effectively.

Bipasha stared, completely mesmerised. She forgot about Samir's skinny chest. She forgot to care about what Yohan would think if he caught her gaping.

Thankfully, Yohan did not pay heed; he sauntered towards the bathroom, whistling away. Before disappearing into the bathroom, he said, 'Won't be a minute, darling…just need to clean myself up.'

Strange! Did he have to do it right now? Did he really have to leave his guest unattended, to cater to his personal grooming? What a peculiar man, Bipasha wondered.

But, yes, there was a difference. The Yohan she had seen so far—at the conferences, in the restaurant, at the party—had no similarity with the Yohan, who had presented himself to her, once they crossed the threshold of this building. That Yohan was a man with a couldn't-care-less attitude. He laughed aloud, cracked crude jokes without a thought and planted a makeshift flag in the snow after a make-believe victory. Students regarded him with awe when he entered a room. That Yohan mingled freely with young girls and teased them without inhibition. But the same Yohan, once he entered his flat, seemed to have shrunk in fear. The man who had appeared to be a free soul, now stood before her as a man with much to hide.

Why wasn't Mirko aware that Yohan's wife and children were away? Why didn't Yohan tell Mirko that his mother, too, was not here? Why didn't he reveal that this was not a home at all?

Well, he had promised to tell her everything soon. She would have him share all his secrets the moment he emerged from his shower.

Bipasha sipped the orange juice and wondered, who was Yohan? Which was the real Yohan?

◄O►

# FIVE

Long ago, Samir had once taken her to visit an aunt of
his in the Sarsuna neighbourhood of Kolkata. That
house too, had been without electricity; a lantern was
the only source of light. An old lady lay on a charpoy
asked in a cracked voice, every now and then, 'Who am
I? Who?'

Samir's aunt, sounding quite helpless, tried to
pacify her, 'Why Ma? You are Brajasundari. You are
your Rajgopal and Brajagopal's mother...'

'Who is Rajgopal? And who is Brajagopal?' The
old woman had exclaimed.

'What? Don't you know your very own Raja
and Braja?'

There had been a hint of anxious fear in Samir's
aunt's voice. Her two grandchildren were crouching

nearby, hugging their knees. Pulling them close she had said, 'Raja and Braja are your sons, Ma!'

'Whose sons? I don't know them...' the cracked voice pierced the darkness again. 'Who am I? Who?'

'You are Brajasundari.'

'Who is this Brajasundari? Which family is she from?'

'Oh God! Have mercy! Let not my worst enemy suffer this fate.' Samir's aunt had joined her palms and, touching them to her forehead, muttered a prayer.

An alien had fear rippled through Bipasha. She had brought with her some rations to help Samir's aunt, who had been a fearless, supporting rock for the boys of their party. Her door was always open for the likes of Samir, Badal, Debu. That very day, three boys had been killed in that area.

This aunt had witnessed the murder of her own son too. And, since then, she had been braving life along with her widowed daughter-in-law and grandchildren.

But, that evening, Bipasha had sensed a strange fear knocking upon this strong woman's heart. The other woman's plea for her own identity did shake one up immensely. Was this the final deal of human destiny—who am I?

Yours truly is Bipasha Choudhury, twenty-five years old, Indo-Anglian poet. The only daughter of Barrister Subarno Choudhury and the sole little sister of IPS Sukanta Choudhury and CA Sujoy Choudhury...

Samir Chatterjee...state prisoner...who are you? Who are you Samir?

Bipasha could hear the shower running in the bathroom. The wall between the two rooms was not ceiling high; the top portion was a glass partition. She also heard Yohan humming to himself.

'Yohan!' Bipasha suddenly called out in a suppressed voice. Since entering this flat, her voice had automatically switched to a stifled mode.

'Coming dear!' Yohan's booming voice replied.

And, almost immediately, Yohan appeared with the white and yellow towel around his waist, his well-toned muscular legs very much on display.

'Sorry, darling. Please excuse my attire.'

Yohan smelt very clean and healthy, almost like a disinfectant, making Bipasha think of a spotless floor cleaned with bleaching powder. But, she thought, the previous sweat-alcohol-fatigue laced lively smell suited Yohan more. All traces of the unkempt Yohan had been washed away to reveal this pristine look.

'The hob does not work without electricity...else I would have made you some coffee.'

'But you can get hot water from the tap.'

'Huh! That won't make proper coffee...that will make Nescaf. We don't drink Nescaf.'

'Not Nescaf...it's called Nescafé.'

'I know...but I like to call it that.' The corners of Yohan's mouth lifted in a smile as he pulled out a chair and sat down.

'Go and change into trousers,' Bipasha said.

'Gosh! I believe, you will not tolerate the barbarian in me at all!'

'No. I don't like wild behaviour.'

'Really? I always thought that women like a touch of wildness.'

'Not me. Go and put on pants like a gentleman, Yohan. You have five minutes.'

'On one condition,' Yohan said with a strange ardour in his voice.

'What condition? Oh, what a fix!'

'You will have to show me how you have draped this long piece of cloth around yourself. Purely scientific interest. I have always been fascinated by unstitched clothing...starting from the Greek era.'

'Is that why you have draped this towel? Something taken from Greek civilisation? Unstitched clothing... of course!'

'Partly that, partly laziness, and partly…' Yohan smiled naughtily.

'What?'

'You can call it mischief.' As he spoke, he stretched out his leg under the table, shook off his slipper and pressed his leg against Bipasha's. Perhaps he sensed the shiver that ran down Bipasha's body because he swiftly blew out the candle and grabbed Bipasha's hand in his large ones.

'To be honest, I am extremely grateful to the electricity department. They have gifted me a wonderful opportunity.'

Bipasha could not rake up a fitting reply. Yohan too, remained silent for a few moments and then said, 'Would you like to get up? Let us go into the other room…'

Bipasha stood up as though in a trance.

Yohan held her hand and led her to some room, a much darker one. When Yohan pulled her into his arms in the corridor, Bipasha's limbs automatically put up their usual well-practised fight. But did her heart resist too? Did her unfaithful body not want to play along?

Bipasha's mind was blank. As she tried to prise her lips away from the warm wet pressure, she realised that they were in a different room.

'Pull the curtains apart, Yohan. Let some light come in.'

Though Bipasha usually preferred the dark, ever since she had walked into this flat, her senses had been craving for a little light like a parched desert traveller. The darkness in this flat was like some trap. Various obscure chapters of Yohan's life seemed to have mingled with it.

Darkness wrapped around her, like underwater weeds. Once, while swimming in a lake in Kolkata, Bipasha's legs had got tangled in underwater weeds and, for an instant, darkness had descended on her senses. But only for an instant. She had immediately managed to struggle and tear away and free herself.

But this darkness was different. She could not fight and tear away from it. It pulled her further and further into its very depths. It had swathed her like the underwater vines. She felt strangled.

'Yo-han, please pull away the curtains.'

Yohan pulled the curtains away and immediately a fragment of the rain-drenched midnight street presented itself to her. A lamp post threw some light towards Bipasha and, for some reason, it appeared to be a lighthouse to her. A promise of light she had suddenly found while floating as a lost soul on the deep dark sea.

In the rain, the light appeared hazy as it lit up the deserted street. A concrete mixer stood in front of a partially built house like some prehistoric monster... bricks were piled at one end...she could not make out what they exactly looked like. In the rain, the light appeared to slip and slide on the shiny and slippery surface of the serpentine dark street.

Mesmerised, Bipasha walked to the window and stood before it, perhaps to inhale deeply and fill her lungs with fresh air. But the thick glass of the window kept the room from mingling with the outside world.

Once the curtains were pulled away, only the indomitable light rushed in and brought with it a medley of meaningless shadows. Sadly, the rain, the fresh air, and the chill did not have permission to enter.

Bipasha pressed her nose to the glass...like a beggar child outside a sweet shop.

Light, fresh air, the street, the rain-soaked night, and the passing moments of life...everything lay on the other side. There wasn't a soul on the street...and surely not in the house under construction.

All of a sudden, two human shadows appeared at one end of the street. Bipasha's heart broke into a joyful dance; the way a peacock spreads its tail and dances at the sight of gathering rain clouds. Awake! They too were awake!

But then, very abruptly, Bipasha felt a pull on her hand and, unable to keep her balance, she stumbled and fell upon Yohan on the floor. Yohan seemed kind of prepared to catch her.

'Uff!' Bipasha exclaimed in an attempt to suppress the pain.

Yohan held her right hand tightly and, instead of apologising, scolded her harshly.

'Don't you dare get up now. Stupid girl! How could you stand at the window like that…that too at this late hour? What will people think?'

Bipasha was stunned.

Where were these people? Who would think what? How would anyone see her in this darkness? The light from the street lamp was surely not enough! What kind of fear was this, which constantly made this man cringe and rage?

Bipasha suddenly recalled the days when Samir and his fellow workers were on the run. A shiver ran through her. Yes, she had seen a far more scary face of fear. The kind of fear that could enrage a man to the point of killing another. A man's deepest fear found strongest release in the face of extreme anger. Bipasha had understood that.

Samir and the other boys spent their nights in a tutorial home. Once, when Samir had been suffering from high fever, Bipasha landed up at the place with some medicine for him. It was a Sunday evening and the tutorial classes were out. Samir had told her not to visit, but she had decided to go ahead anyway.

Samir had opened the door and pulled her in... quite like Yohan. And no sooner was she inside, he landed a resounding slap on her cheek. Her ears buzzed and her head reeled. Humiliation, hurt, and disbelief had stunned her.

But, then too, she had been unable to cry. Samir had gritted his teeth and said, 'Stupid, idiot...immature girl! Won't listen to anything! They are right...you will land us in trouble, Bipasha. You and that swine of a brother of yours.'

Apparently, the police were at a close range. Samir had warned her not to visit again, not to meet him again. It seemed, her brother had set spies on her.

He had lashed out at her with suppressed anger in his voice, 'Don't you dare visit me again till I ask you to. Your immaturity will expose all our shelters in no time! It's sad but...perhaps the women of this country are not yet ready to be part of revolution. Don't you have a single serious bone in you? I had warned you time and again...don't you even realise a situation of life and death? How can you be so shallow... so disgusting?'

At that, Bipasha had broken down. But Samir did not pay any heed to it. He did not attempt to coax and cajole her to stop crying. Instead, he sat aloof, smoking away and nursing his grudge. Eventually, he said, 'My mistake! How could I expect a rich, bourgeois brat like you to understand what a revolution is all about? Subarno Choudhury is a fraud who fights for the industrialist Birlas...one of his sons is a murderer in the guise of police, while the other son is a cheating CA. What can one expect of such a man's daughter? How different can she be? It's my mistake!'

In a flash, something had exploded in her head. Volcanic rage had erupted within her. Perhaps a reshuffle of her stars occurred at that very moment, and Bipasha said, 'Very well. I will now be what you take me to be. I will drag you all into the dumps. I will reveal everything to my brother...right away. I will be whatever you have accused me of being.'

There was none at the tutorial that day. Sensing that things may have gone too far, Samir had immediately pacified her, caressed, and appeased her.

Bipasha, unable to hold away for long, had ultimately surrendered herself to his aroused and fevered body.

A while later, fatigued by fear and love, Samir had perhaps dozed off. Bipasha had taken the opportunity to slip away silently when she opened the door for Badal.

And that was the end.

The sky crashed on them that very day. Bipasha was not the one who let the cat out, the Almighty was her witness. She could very well be a fool—she had desired love more than revolution—but she was not a traitor.

Samir, believe me, I knew nothing.

That night, the police raided their hideout while Samir was away; Badal and Debu were arrested.

After that, the chain of events unfolded at an alarming pace. Quite like a fast-paced comic strip from the soundless era of motion pictures. Bipasha's brother informed their father that his boss had received Samir's kit bag as evidence from Prof. Anupam Roy. It had bombs, a pipe-gun, a book on Mao, as well as Samir's notebook. And, love letters from Bipasha.

Without wasting a moment, Bipasha's father had flown to Mumbai with her, that very night. Her passport was made in haste there, and within ten days she was bundled off to London. While at Mumbai, Bipasha received news that Samir had been arrested.

'Bipasha?' Someone called her from far away.

'Hm?' Bipasha responded.

'I am sorry. I shouldn't have spoken to you in that way. Please don't mind...say something. Why are you not speaking? Scold me...!'

'I did not mind at all,' Bipasha said and made a futile attempt to sit up.

Yohan was lying on his back, and Bipasha lay partially on top of him, imprisoned by his strong arms.

Gosh! Where had her good senses eloped to? Did they abandon her completely? She had not realised that she was literally spread-eagled over a male chest!

Oh Samir! Take a look at the rich, bourgeois brat...! Bipasha tried to break free forcefully as she said in irritation, 'Yohan, let go...please leave me. I don't like this at all...please...'

But Yohan showed no signs of listening to her plea.

Bipasha felt extremely uncomfortable. She bit out her next words in a cold voice, 'Now I will scream.'

She had hit the right chord. Yohan released her in a flash, as if struck by lightning.

Bipasha lifted herself up. Rearranging her clothes, she settled with her back against the wall, her knees drawn up to her chest. Yohan too sat up.

'They are security personnel and extremely vigilant. They know that my wife is not here. In fact, everyone here knows that my wife is in Hungary. What if they had seen you at the window?'

'Then what? Can't people have guests? In this country, are female guests not allowed to visit if your wife is not home?'

'I hold a responsible position, Bipasha. I am the Chief Secretary of this chapter of the party. I am always in public eye. I don't have a private life, it must be an open book. Nitra is a small provincial town, and the people too, are of narrow mindset. Not everyone is like Mirko. The social norms are very conservative and strict, Bipasha. The same as in most small towns.'

'So, if a woman visits you on a odd day...'

'Oh no!' Yohan interrupted with a tut-tut, attempting to correct her misconception. Then he continued, 'It's not that easy...this is not one of your permissive societies of Western Europe. This is a socialist state where morality is a big thing. And it has loomed larger after 1986, in an attempt to stop bourgeois infiltration. During my student days, I have never seen the kind of discipline, which has come into force now in the name of counter-revolution. Bipasha, I don't think you understand. To be honest, your kind...Indians who write poetry in English...will not understand these things.'

Again, something flashed in Bipasha's head and anger erupted. Volcanic anger. This is what men usually did when arrested by fear and helplessness—humiliate the weakest person close at hand. Bipasha counselled herself to tame her rage. No, she would never again surrender to vicious rage. She ordered herself not to retaliate...perhaps, try and change the topic.

'Does your mother know that your wife is not in Hungary?'

'No, I haven't told her.'

'Why?'

'She is well into her years and a communist at heart...she still likes to dream. She is working very hard because she would like to leave behind an ideal socialist state for her grandchildren.'

'How are these two things connected?'

Tenderly, he took Bipasha's hand in his. Then he gazed out the window and said, 'They won't be coming back, Bipasha.'

'What do you mean?'

'I mean…' Yohan bit down on his lip.

Bipasha realised that an immense turmoil of sorts was raging within him. She now accepted Yohan's hands into the fold of her own and applied some comforting pressure. As though to lend him courage, the way a soldier would to his wounded comrade.

Yohan revealed, 'My wife has left me, Bipasha. Well, not really me…more my motherland and my party. She loathes them. But can someone who hates my party and my Czechoslovakia love me as an individual? No…I cannot imagine such a relationship between two close people.'

He continued, 'Tell me, how do I reveal to Mirko that Katrina has left? How do I tell him that she has spat in the face of my country and my dreams and left for good? I have lost, Bipasha. This is my biggest defeat as a human being. How can a man, who couldn't convince his wife, instil belief in the hearts of his countrymen? Can you tell me where the fruit of my lifelong work lies?'

Bipasha didn't know what to say to him. At a loss for words, the only way she could offer comfort was to pull his hands onto her lap.

'My sons will not return. Katrina has written, 'I have brought my sons to a free life!' The silly girl…

after all her struggles, she has not yet realised where freedom lies! Is freedom really in Paris? Can capitalism ever provide freedom?

'Katrina does not know what a soup she has landed my sons in...what a life of servility she has burdened them with. Is this freedom? Tell me, Bipasha. The very poison that my mother and I have struggled lifelong to destroy has now been introduced into the lives of my sons by Katrina. My mother is sixty-five...I could not bring myself to reveal this to her, Bipasha. She bought the bunk bed for her grandsons, decorated the walls with colourful posters...she is doing up the room for them. I cannot bear to tell her that her grandsons will never sleep in those beds...perhaps, she will never see them again.'

Bipasha asked, 'Why? Can't she visit them in Paris?'

'Maybe...maybe not. Can't say for sure.'

'I think the boys will return. They will return to their own country, once they grow up.'

'Can't say, Bipasha. Can't say anything for sure. The venom of capitalism is very powerful, it destroys a man's resistance completely. It gnaws at the roots of his values and even sours the very soil he survives on. Luxury is a contagious evil, extremely nasty. I have learnt from my personal experiences with Katrina.'

Yohan appeared to be speaking in a trance. His eyes were not on Bipasha, but she could feel his hands groping for some more comfort. Bipasha held Yohan's large hands in her tiny delicate ones, resting them on her drawn up knees close to her chest. Yet, she could sense that Yohan's hands craved further comfort; they hungered for a warmer haven. Oh dear! What should she do now?

Quite anxious with the situation, Bipasha said, 'What's the time, Yohan? I really must leave now.'

'Not yet...please stay for a little longer, dear. I am very lonely here. There is no one I can talk to. Not only today, I never had someone I could talk to since the time I matured. Katrina was never interested in what I needed to say, and there are things I can no longer share with my mother. I am still young, and I am a man...I like to shield my mother from all difficulties. But how do I shield myself? Tell me...'

Did the cat run away with her tongue? Why couldn't she speak? Could she truly not guess what Yohan really wanted of her? She had spent ten years as a single woman in the permissive society of writers and creative people where morals were flippant.

Samir's Bipasha would have perhaps been ignorant but this Bipasha was different.

'I can't take it anymore. Bipasha, please have mercy on me. My body, my heart, my entire life…everything is parched…have mercy. Believe me, Bipasha, there is no sin in this. Why don't you consider this to be a charity? You have in abundance…why can't you spare some and be magnanimous? You have nothing to lose by quenching the thirst of a few like me.'

Yohan had stuffed his face between Bipasha's knees. Bipasha suddenly realised that his arms had crept around her, holding her doll-like little body tightly.

No words registered with her. The only thing she was aware of was the strong and pungent smell of fresh paint; it made her feel heady. She slipped into a daze and rested a hand on Yohan's head. And instantly, Yohan grabbed the hand and smothered it with countless restive kisses.

'My darling…oh, my dear…my grasshopper… my dream from a faraway land…'

Bipasha sat still as a stone statue. Yohan had forcibly pushed his face into her bosom and was now moaning in a feeble and fevered voice, 'You are so beautiful, Bipasha…you are so beautiful. Are you a dream, Bipasha…are you a dream? Tell me, am I dreaming?'

Bipasha had no clue how to recognise and respect this moment of surrender. Her hands pulled Yohan's restless head closer to her chest, the way a mother would draw close a frightened child and comfort him. There was no scope for rational thoughts. In such moments, the human body preferred to determine its own travel path, take its own decisions.

These primal natural tendencies were inborn, and hence, usually flawless. In those moments, common sense played truant. Humans did not have the time to ponder over the norms of civilisation; they did not spare the time to tally up the dos and don'ts of the past and the future. One did not have the time to erect walls and so, nature took over and made the honest, the precise, and the inevitable happen. The way one raises one's hands to defend himself when someone lifts a dagger to him; or, the way our legs move in reflex when a particular point on our knees is hit with an orthopaedic hammer.

Following the course of such inevitability, Bipasha closed her eyes.

Samir, that day you…in a similar manner, you had…we were still very young, weren't we, Samir? We were quite naive and unaware; you were a very cautious young man…yet, that day, you behaved in a similar manner, didn't you, Samir? That day, when you were burning with fever…didn't we, Samir? Yet, now, I don't even know which prison you are in, Presidency or Purulia. Come closer Samir…caress me…don't be angry anymore, Samir. Believe me, I was not at fault… I did not tell my brother anything. I didn't even know that you had left your kit bag with Prof. Roy. How surprising! How could a man like him stoop so low? But then, fear had extreme power, like a cobra's venom. There was nothing that fear couldn't compel a man to do; fear was well capable of making Prof. Roy behave in that way. Fear, which made you say all those things to your Bipasha; fear, which keeps me in London even after all these years; fear, which made me…fear, which made Yohan…

'Yohan, please leave me. I need to go home… please let me go. I am scared, I am extremely scared… Oh, Yohan!'

How deep, how green, how densely dark was this  forest, cavernous, long—the moss laden trees touching each other on top, making endless gateways after gateways, like pairs of palms in salutation, like the gothic arches of a church. Fresh young leaves sprouted on trees, in the coiling twines budded new flowers. From hidden quarters came twittering of the birds—yet, how surprising—the forest floor had so much snow, so much snow, ah the snows of yesteryear! The more you trod, the deeper you sank. Deeper and deeper. Will this forest never get any light, any air? Right then, cracking the ice, suddenly and miraculously, one proud blue crocus sprang, singing the glory of spring. Someone whispered in a sunny airy voice—'We have conquered this peak together—this crocus is our flag of victory.'

Opening her eyes Bipasha saw in front of her the vast expansive glass pane, freckled with raindrops—its shadow reflected along the wall looked like measles—does even water have such a shadow? Bipasha, noticed for the first time. How amazing this world was.

'Bipasha?'

'Yes?'

'I don't know what kind of an impression you got of me—I only wish to say, what you gave me today is the most precious treasure, in my forty-one years.'

'You are talking like a capitalist.'

'Yes I am a capitalist, when it comes to memories.'

Samir too had said—'I have a petty bourgeoisie mentality about you. You are my property...my private property.'

Bipasha didn't feel like speaking. Turning her hand she took a quick glance at her watch, and promptly sat up.

Seeing her up, Yohan got up as well. He flickered the lighter, to look at his watch

'I will be back,' he said and went out. He came back immediately, 'Come, do you want to go?'

Bipasha stood up. She flapped her saree and started tying it up.

Yohan quickly added, 'Wait, wait, I want to see how you tie around so much of material…'

Bipasha ignores him. 'I want to drink some water.'

'Surely—Come, I will give you.' Then placed his hand around her shoulder and asked, 'Did you like it?'

The intervening few seconds quivered. Like veins on the temple, darkness throbbed.

Bipasha turned her head in one direction rather listlessly. This unnecessary question posed by men forever had only one answer. The lingering shadows of the raindrops turned blurry in her eyes, till they melded and took shape of a dark cloud. She turned her palm and wiped her eyes. At once, the measles-freckled raindrop shadow re-appeared on the glass-pane. Bipasha smiled to herself. Ah, if only those shadows of droplets could be gathered to get a raincloud.

Tucking his shirt into the waistband of his trousers, Yohan said, 'Will you keep a request of mine, Bipasha?'

'Oh dear! Another request?'

This made Yohan laugh and he said, 'Truly, you are a very mischievous girl! I will miss you terribly. Tomorrow, at this time, you will be far, far away. Perhaps you will have forgotten me by then.'

Bipasha steered away from such talk and said, 'Come on, tell me what request you have in mind... quick! Will keep it if possible.'

'I'd like to give you two letters. Will you please post them for me in London?'

A siren blared in Bipasha's head, alerting her of impending danger. Her features hardened.

'What kind of letters? I can't take such responsibility unless I am aware of their content. I am a guest in this country, and I am not ready to be the bearer of any misfortune for this land, knowingly or unknowingly.'

For an instant, Yohan was baffled by Bipasha's stern voice and harsh words but then, in the very next instant, he lifted her off the ground, with much pomp, and kissed her resoundingly.

'*Sagesse d'un poete, je t'envie*. Bipasha, you could have been a communist of the first order...what amazing values and dedication you have! Wish my Katrina was like you.'

Now it was Bipasha's turn to be surprised. But her ears were ablaze with that one sentence—you could have been a communist of the first order! The words rang in a repeat loop in her mind, scorching her consciousness. Samir, did you hear what they are saying? That I could be....

'One is a professional one, academic...and the other is for my wife. The letters are nothing much. Let me show you.'

Yohan fetched his briefcase and put it on the kitchen table. Then he took out two envelopes from within. One had an incomplete address on it— a professor's name, the house number, and the road name. The city and the country names were missing. From within the envelope, Yohan took out a letter and a photocopy of some article.

'Why are you not posting this here? What is the problem?'

'Once you are in London, write Seoul and South Korea on this envelope. Did you get that? We can't post to Seoul from here...prohibited region. This professor does some work in my field of study so, I want him to read this article of mine, which has been translated into English.'

'How surprising! And the other one?'

'Here. This has the address on it but not the recipient's name. You write it…write Katrina followed by my last name. The letter is in French. You can read it if you want.'

'Huh? Don't you write to your wife in your own language?'

'Do we have a common language? She is Hungarian and I am Slovak. Though, of course, each of us knows the other's language quite well. Yet, our written communication is in French, and Katrina is the one responsible for this. Katrina and her feudal family background…they have been taught since childhood that written communication should be either in German or in French. Now, since German is more of a commoner's language, French happens to be more elite. And, Katrina always likes to be on the classier side.'

'Then where is the problem in me writing poetry in English? Why would you call that colonial servility?'

'But this is the same! Did I say that this was any different? Bipasha, our socialism is yet to mature.

It is still riddled with countless controversies and contradictions. And, to hide ourselves from that world, we adopt various safety measures. Yet, let me tell you, in spite of all these flaws and imperfections, a day will dawn when true socialism will reign in this country...yes, it will. It cannot be any other way. The dedication and hard work of so many people for so many years cannot be in vain. These instances of hide-and-seek, this shroud of conspiracy have been with us since the time of Stalin...but they cannot be with us forever. Things will change. There will come a time when letters will be posted to Seoul from Nitra... when a man will not have to hang his head in shame if his wealthy wife decides to relocate to Paris.'

Yohan laughed in an easy manner as he spoke. Bipasha pondered in amazement, just a little while ago, on this very night, the same problem had sat like an extremely heavy burden on this man. Was it possible that with the little he had received from her, in this short time, the burden was lifted? Could that little bit change a man so?

All of a sudden, Yohan lifted Bipasha, threw her into the air and caught her back with ease. 'Grasshopper, you are like a little doll, almost weightless. Gosh! If only my neighbours could see us together! It saddens me to think that no one will ever know how destiny smiled on me today.'

Back on the ground, Bipasha stuffed the letters into her bag and held up the candle. 'Not a minute more. Look Yohan, it is thirty-five past three. Bechka will come to pick me up at five.'

'Oh well! Listen, don't go telling Bechka that you were here for so long! If she asks…which she will, being a farmer's daughter, unlike Yanka and Evichka, and quite simple-minded…tell her that you left this place at one. Otherwise, tomorrow…'

'I know, I know.' Bipasha assured him and walked towards the coat closet. Near the cupboard, she noticed the flower tub waiting beside the shoes. Mirko's tulips…three bright red ones. The darkness in this flat seemed to have grown on her in these few hours, it seemed quite familiar. The smell of fresh paint too had invaded her heart and found place. She felt as though this flat has been home to her for ages. She picked up the flower tub and held it to her chest.

It was drizzling when they walked out onto the deserted street, not a soul or a vehicle was in sight. Yohan pulled up the hood of his coat over his head and said, 'Let's see if we can get a taxi. I have a hood but you are getting wet.'

'I too have a hood, though not with my coat...' Bipasha said as she covered her head with the free end of her saree.

On the street, the pile of bricks, the half-built house, the rows of parked cars, and the lamp posts seemed happy to see them together. On one side, an ancient tree stood silent witness to life around, bearing the burden of darkness on its head and getting drenched in the rain. Yohan held the flower tub in one hand, and his other hand loosely wrapped around Bipasha's waist. As they walked, he kicked at the odd stone or pebble every now and then, like a seasoned footballer.

'Aren't you afraid someone might see us now?' Bipasha asked in wonder.

'Oh no, this is not the time for the security guards to patrol.'

All of a sudden, the sound of a lively chorus reached them. At that juncture, the street took a bend, and it seemed as if a group was approaching from the other end. Noticing a couple of men in hats coming their way, Yohan promptly shoved the flower tub into Bipasha's hands. And then, without awarding her any time to collect her thoughts or wits, he swiftly gathered her into his arms and claimed her lips with his. Bipasha almost choked, and an abrupt fear welled up inside her—this was not a usual kiss, this was something else!

The chorus passed by them. Someone from the group whistled and another passed a remark. The others laughed loudly.

Feeling trapped, Bipasha tried to wriggle free but the flower tub hampered her efforts. Realising her intention, Yohan tightened his arms around her. Till the chorus faded away completely, their entwined form remained unmoving, throwing a hazy and formless shadow on the pavement. And beside it, on the rain drenched street, was the swaying shadow of the tulips.

Raindrops fell on Bipasha's lips. Her eyes too were damp.

Releasing Bipasha, Yohan said, 'Sorry, Bipasha, a group of drunk labourers returning home. Seemed like they are from my chapter. Had I not done that, they would have recognised me. By doing this, I somehow managed to hide my face...do you understand? Moreover, they were drunk. Who knows what they would have done if they had noticed you standing here in your unusual attire. Drunkards are neither communist nor capitalist. I guess, this also served to protect you. Wasn't it a good idea? What do you say?'

Flabbergasted by the bizarre justification, Bipasha asked in awe, 'Are there drunkards even in a socialist state?'

Yohan laughed and replied, 'I should say no... but, what do you think?'

Upon reaching the gates of the women's hostel Yohan bid her farewell with only a peck on each cheek, mainly because a robust guardswoman sat vigil in the tiny kiosk by the gate.

Then he lowered his voice and said, 'We shall meet again, Bipasha...we surely will. The world is a small place and life too big...this is only the beginning! This is not our last meeting, Bipasha. Mark my words, this is nothing but the first of many more to come.'

Bipasha kept quiet. Then she mechanically raised her right hand and waved a goodbye. Her left hand was wrapped around the flower tub. The corpulent guardswoman said something to which Yohan replied. Bipasha understood neither.

Yohan said, 'Go on, Bipasha, go upstairs. She is not happy with us loitering here. We shall meet again, but *partir c'est un peu de mourir*...each parting is like a little of death. Bipasha...my little green grasshopper....'

Bidding goodbye to Yohan, Bipasha was about to go inside when something struck her and she turned around. Then she ran towards the gate and called out, 'Yohan!'

Yohan halted in his tracks abruptly, quite surprised. Then he too turned around and asked, 'Yes, my darling?'

'Take this, Yohan. Take it home. This is a present for you, from your grasshopper.' Bipasha held out the tulip sapling, with its vibrant flowers, towards Yohan. The plant seemed to lend an assurance that it would flower through the spring and brighten up days.

Without a word, Yohan accepted the plant.

Mirko's song played in her head as Bipasha climbed the stairs to the third floor, fatigue weighing her down. The building was huge with numerous rooms, and students roamed in their nightwear. Even at this late hour, the place was buzzing with life.

Entering her room, Bipasha realised that it was already twenty-five past four. Bechka would arrive soon. She needed to pack the suitcase immediately; but, instead, Bipasha walked out to the balcony attached to the room.

Below, the wide road rolled away into the wee hours of the morning. In the distance, she noticed a tall shadowy figure, the hood pulled over his head, walking away along the deserted street as the rain washed over him. His hands were gathered to his chest as though he was carefully carrying some divine treasure.

Bipasha returned to the room, took off her coat and switched on the radiator. The faint whirring from the radiator broke the lonely silence of the room. She sat on the bed for a while, her hands gathered on her lap, and tried to sort through her feelings and comprehend what had happened. But her mind felt devoid of anything coherent, her heart was in no mood to participate in any logical discussion. So, Bipasha turned her attention away from the confusion within and focussed on the job at hand.

Though the clock proclaimed that night was over, the scene outside refuted it. Through the glass doors, Bipasha saw the rain-drenched night sky of Nitra reclining in eternal sleep atop the foliage.

But Bipasha did not have time to catch a few winks, or even relax. She had to leave soon. As she packed her bits and bobs into the suitcase, she thought how nice it would be if Bechka did not come to fetch her and just sent the car over. Though Bechka had become a friend in the past eight days, right now she would prefer not to face her.

There was a knock on the door.

'Come in, Bechka.'

'Hey! You are ready! All dressed and bed made, I see. You are a very efficient girl...my mother would have been happy to meet you.'

True, the unused bed was made up to perfection, the clean sheets stretched and tucked neatly. Bipasha spared a glance towards it, but then looked away.

'I would have loved to meet your mother. But you did not arrange for it, did you?'

Bechka instantly flushed red as an apple in embarrassment. 'What could I do? Everything was planned by Yohan. I really wanted to take you home and show you a farm.'

As she spoke, she opened her bag and fished out two apples, quite like her own face. 'My father has sent these for you...these are from our tree.'

'Wow! Thank you, Bechka...thank you. Your father doesn't even know me, yet he has sent these for me with so much care.'

Bipasha's mood lifted. Not that she liked apples much; but still, she felt kind of happy. But, was it really joy? Or was it sorrow? Suddenly, she felt a sharp pang seize her heart.

'Let me quickly wash my face...' she said and hurried to the wash basin by the door. Then, as she splashed water over her face with her cupped hands, she let the tears flow freely, crying her heart out. But silently. If there was one thing this room didn't have, it was privacy. There were no curtains, no doors, and Bechka was in the room. There was no refuge for tears.

Bipasha continued to splash water over her face. Samir, oh Samir, where have I got myself into, all alone? Nowadays, I cannot comprehend anything. Is this sadness? Am I sad because I have to leave Yohan? But I don't even know the man properly. In that case, is this feeling for you, Samir? A dull pain is rising from my heart, twisting and turning through it…what pain is this? Samir, please explain to me what this pain is about.

Yohan had said that this was not the end; it was but the beginning. But what was to become of a girl who could not even differentiate between a beginning and an end? Where would she find herself in this world?

The sound of a train's whistle floated to Bipasha from far away. A train seemed to rumble over a bridge on its journey towards distant places. Samir, please tell me which way I am to go…

Bipasha felt like banging her head against the white cold wash basin, which had a stark antiseptic look and feel. But Bechka was in the room.

Since childhood, our father has misguided us. All the beliefs projected by my brothers were wrong. Everything was wrong, Samir. Perhaps, if my mother had been alive, she would have led me along the right path…but, who knows! The pain in my heart is unbearable…the miles and miles of barren stretches in my heart confuse me. Which way do I go? Which way is home?

'Bipasha, you'll catch a cold. Come away from the water now,' Bechka called out. 'And get ready. It's raining hard so we'll have to keep time in hand for the journey. Also, I heard that a storm is on the way.'

'A storm! Along with this rain?'

'Yes, it's quite usual in March and April.'

Bipasha put her coat on and picked up the suitcase. Before leaving the room, she glanced around to check if she was leaving anything behind. Perhaps an odd fragment of the poet Bipasha Choudhury?

Bechka reached out towards the radio and turned it off. Bipasha switched the light off and, immediately, the darkness outside and the darkness inside flowed and mingled into each other. Bechka pulled the door shut and kept the keys with her. Then she snatched Bipasha's suitcase from her saying, 'Come on, give it to me. You are a grasshopper, you won't be able to manage.'

A storm was brewing. Along with heavy rain, the winds had picked up.

Bechka munched on apples, one after another, saving the seeds in her coat pocket. Bipasha, though, was still nibbling on the single apple as the car sped along.

'What make is this car? Is it a Mercedes Benz?'

'No, not a Mercedes, but you can call this a Russian equivalent. A very good car.'

'I can make out as much. It's quite a soundless and smooth ride, very comfortable.'

Fields, farms, and the occasional factory raced past them on either side. Small villages and provincial towns rushed away in extreme hurry.

The rain and the wind strove to outdo each other as they increased in intensity. The road was devoid of trees so, Bipasha could not make out how strong the wind actually was. But, every now and then the air-tight car, with all its windows rolled up, trembled against the force of the wind, as though it was struggling to keep itself from turning over. The stormy weather kept the sky in darkness and morning was yet to find a way to break in.

'Visibility is so low that we cannot drive any faster,' Bechka said. A government employed chauffeur, in khaki uniform, was driving them.

'Yes, moreover, one cannot speed up in this strong wind,' Bipasha added.

'There isn't much time till your bus leaves.'

'We did leave on time, though.'

'Yes, but now it seems we should have kept more time in hand. I didn't realise that the storm would build up so much.'

Bechka vented her anxiety, and Bipasha kept the conversation going. Yet, she felt unable to genuinely share Bechka's anxiety. Though, Bechka's worry was completely for her sake! She felt very guilty for the disconnect she was experiencing. Of late, nothing seemed to be able to excite her.

If she was late, she would miss the bus to Vienna. If she missed the bus, she would fail to catch her flight to London. That was all, wasn't it? Fine, no big deal. There would be other buses and other flights. This was not the end. What was the extreme worry for? Bipasha felt, nothing in life was worth being very attached to or being extremely involved with. Surely, catching a flight was not a matter of life and death! But then...Bipasha, do you really have any matter of life and death at hand?

Bipasha, where will you be going if you can catch this flight? Will you be going home? Where are you headed? What flight is it that you are hurrying to catch? Where are you going in this rainy, windy morning of dark clouds and wild storm? Where are you coming from and where are you destined? Can you call this a return journey, at all? From Nitra to London...from square one to square one. How will you be able to tally your life? Bipasha was lost in a silent conversation with herself.

Bechka asked something a couple of times, and then she too, fell silent in the absence of a reply.

Thousands of words raced towards Bipasha, willing to take over her mind and heart. Scores and scores of piercing questions aimed for her...like the spear-headed raindrops, fearlessly riding the furious wind. Bipasha felt helpless.

Bechka's voice did not reach her. She thought, where am I going? Into the vast, free world? But where? You are on your way to London, to write poetry in English. Bipasha, won't you go home?

Samir, you used to pull my leg because I wrote to you in English. But I never got around to learning my mother tongue in school. Samir, I won't write to you in English ever again, I promise...I swear. Do you know, Samir, even Yohan is more of a free bird than I am. The Yohan, who is pained by incomplete dreams and torn apart by futile anxiety. I am sure, you too are still indomitable, though behind bars. Yohan too, is completely free, even in the shadows of imperfect ideals. Because...you have the unfettered earth beneath, you have your mother tongue, your motherland. Your soil holds the promise of bounteous spring. Oh Samir, which lonely forest have I wandered into? I want to go home. This time, I will surely return home. Samir, I will certainly find you.

Look at Yohan, he lives in his own home. Yes, his life may be riddled with sorrows and pain, but he is at peace. Who knows where Katrina lost herself? I don't want to lose myself like Katrina. I want to go home, Samir. Yohan, though a communist, could easily say, 'We shall meet again, Bipasha...we surely will. The world is a small place and life too big...this is only the beginning! This is not our last meeting...' Yet, I know very well that there will not be any need in future for me to return to this non-descript little town of Czechoslovakia. Yohan too, must be aware of the same... yet, he could promise. Believe me, Samir, I feel I will be able to return. I will not cower in fear anymore. At last, I have found my way home...now, I will return home, Samir. Let it pour, let the storm rage, let problems crowd around us...we will surely be able to make the new green-sprouts flower...every season will be spring for us....

'Bipasha?' Bechka gently pulled at her arm. 'We have reached Bratislava. There is your bus stop. We are about five minutes late but the bus hasn't left yet. You can still catch it if you make a dash.'

'The bus is still here?' Bipasha cried out, as if shaken awake abruptly.

'Yes, yes, we are very lucky.'

'Let's run...' Carrying Bipasha's suitcase, Bechka started to run in the rain. Bipasha too, followed with short hurried steps, holding the pleats of her saree off the ground.

Once on the bus, she peeked out from behind the window curtain. In the pouring rain, the busy five-point crossing looked like the rain drenched Chowringhee-Dharmatala crossing of Kolkata.

—◄o►—